PURRFECT MATCH

THE MYSTERIES OF MAX 54

NIC SAINT

PURRFECT MATCH

The Mysteries of Max 54

Copyright © 2022 by Nic Saint

All rights reserved. No part of this book may be reproduced in any form by any electronic or mechanical means including photocopying, recording, or information storage and retrieval without permission in writing from the author.

This is a work of fiction. Names, characters, places, brands, media, and incidents are either the product of the author's imagination or are used fictitiously. The author acknowledges the trademarked status and trademark owners of various products referenced in this work of fiction, which have been used without permission. The publication/use of these trademarks is not authorized, associated with, or sponsored by the trademark owners.

Edited by Chereese Graves

www.nicsaint.com

Give feedback on the book at: info@nicsaint.com

facebook.com/nicsaintauthor
@nicsaintauthor

First Edition

Printed in the U.S.A

PURRFECT MATCH

Cats à la Mode

When you've lived with humans for as long as I have, you learn to take the bad with the good. The good being a nice home, decent grub and a daily ration of cuddles (though never enough, of course—never enough). So what's the bad? Having to accompany your humans when they go on a matchmaking mission to try and bring together two sundered hearts. Gran and Scarlett had decided to take their Dear Gabi agony column on the road, and go undercover where their Dear Readers were, to try and fix what was broken—and even some of the things that weren't.

And so Dooley and I found ourselves at Advantage Publishing, publisher of magazines like *Glimmer*, *Vigor*, *Fish & Tackle*, and of course *Cat Life*. Gran and Scarlett as senior interns, and Dooley and I as their emotional support animals. The people who'd written to Dear Gabi were Natalie Ferrara, who was expecting her boss's baby, and had recently been unceremoniously dumped by the man, and Tom Mitchell, who was in love with a colleague, but found his affections not reciprocated. Office romance, in other words. Not exactly my strong suit! Lucky for us, before long a murder was committed, and even as 'Gabi' continued to work her magic, I found myself shifting into detective mode.

And then of course there were some odds and ends, like Tex accidentally redistributing his old love letters to Marge around the neighborhood, causing her no small measure of embarrassment. And Harriet being in line for a photo shoot for the cover of *Cat Life*, resulting in a lot of hullaballoo when she woke up one morning to discover a spot on her nose.

CHAPTER 1

The atmosphere in the offices of the Advantage Publishing Company was as electric as ever. The publisher of such well-known publications as *Glimmer*, *Glitter* and *Vigor*—the magazine for the virile man—was considered by friend and foe as a regular powerhouse of the publishing industry. But with the diminished returns publishers saw on their print portfolio these days, and the ongoing transition to digital, tensions were running high in the hallowed halls of publishing. And nowhere was this more apparent than at the desk of Natalie Ferrara, located next to the corner office occupied by Advantage bigwig and CEO Michael Madison.

Natalie had been Mike Madison's personal assistant for going on five years, and in that time had fallen for her handsome boss's charms in a major way. So much so that she now found herself in trouble. Big trouble.

She was an attractive young woman of twenty-seven, with shiny hair the color of honey, cornflower-blue eyes and the kind of face and figure that could launch a thousand ships. What it hadn't managed, though, was to induce

Michael Madison to divorce Mrs. Madison and make an honest woman out of his mistress.

Natalie pressed a tissue to her eyes. She was feeling particularly leaky again, and much to her embarrassment could not stop crying. If Mike saw her like this...

Oh, who was she kidding? Her boss's affections for her had taken a major dive in recent weeks. In fact she could pinpoint the exact date Natalie Ferrara stock had crashed and burned: when she had announced that she was pregnant, and that in due course a baby was going to be born who, if it was a boy, would no doubt inherit his daddy's firm jawline and no-nonsense attitude to life and business, and if it was a girl, hopefully would look more like her mother.

Contrary to what Natalie had expected, or secretly hoped, Michael had reacted to the news in the worst possible way, and had told her what he thought of the future prospects of his offspring by giving her the name of an excellent abortion clinic, offering to pay for the termination. He'd even said she could have the week off, and had grinned and clearly expected her to show her gratefulness by yipping with joy and throwing her arms around his neck and showering him with kisses.

Instead, she'd spent the entire weekend crying her eyes out, and now, two weeks later, she was still crying.

The fact that her brother Luke chose this exact moment to show up on her doorstep and foist his obnoxious personality on her, only added to her distress.

Loud noises emanating from Michael's office tore her away from her musings on the terrible fate that had befallen her, and for a moment her hand hovered over the phone, ready to call security.

Howard White, the well-known designer and *enfant terrible* of the fashion world, had had his run-ins with Michael before, but today sounded worse than usual.

"How dare you!" the eccentric fashion icon screamed. "You, sir, are a louse, a nitwit, a parasite, sucking the blood of the real talent: me! And you dare to criticize me? Me?!"

Natalie's hand relaxed. She really couldn't imagine Howard actually getting physical with Michael, who was a full head taller than he was, twenty-five years younger, and had about thirty pounds on the man, all hard-packed muscle, as she knew from personal experience.

Suddenly the door to the CEO's office swung open and a furious Howard stormed out. He was dressed in one of his own creations: a colorful kaftan hemmed with gold thread. His assistant Sebastian Lipskey was also with him. Neither of the men offered her a single glance as they passed her desk. Then they were gone. And good riddance, too, as far as Natalie was concerned.

Michael appeared at the door, his smoothly shaven face working as he watched the departure of the fashion mogul. He gave Natalie a pointed look, and grunted, "My office, Miss Ferrara. Now!"

And once again Natalie found herself scurrying into the CEO's office. Only this time probably not for a quick session of hot nookie.

꽃

Tom Mitchell, who sat two desks behind Natalie, watched the secretary's hurried entry into Madison's inner realm. Unlike the CEO, he had noticed Natalie's red eyes and her tears, no matter how hard she tried to hide them under a thick layer of makeup. Clearly the girl was in trouble, and even though the source of her trouble was unknown to Tom, Natalie's visible distress weighed heavily on him.

For Tom had some trouble of his own to deal with,

namely his unrequited affections for the golden-haired secretary, which had been plaguing him from the moment he'd started work at Advantage three years ago. All this time he'd been admiring the lovely young woman from afar, knowing she would never be his.

It had been made clear to him from day one to whom Natalie's affections in fact belonged: her affair with the big boss wasn't exactly a big secret. And many was the time he'd seen her sneak into his office, the blinds being pulled, the door being locked, and certain sounds emanating from the office that were more appropriate in a nature documentary than in the offices of a prominent CEO.

Then again, Michael Madison, as far as Tom had been able to ascertain, ticked all the boxes of your classic industry chieftain: he was brash, overconfident, narcissistic, uber-ambitious, and had a wandering eye and ditto hands.

But even though this affair had pretty much sunk Natalie's stock amongst her fellow staffers, it hadn't put a dent in Tom's secret affections. That young man's heart had belonged to Natalie from the moment he first laid eyes on her, and as far as he was concerned, would always remain that way, now and forever.

But since no one likes to wait for now or even forever, he decided to put pen to paper—or rather fingers to keyboard—and pour his heart out in a message to Hampton Cove's favorite agony column. And so he began: 'Dear Gabi...'

❦

Three rows behind Tom, Doris Booth sat silently fuming as she stared at the gift Michael had left on her desk that morning. It was a copy of Strunk & White's *Elements of Style*. The perfect gift for anyone struggling with the basic tenets of grammar and spelling.

As the main publicist for *Glimmer*, language was Doris's forte. It was her secret weapon and her proudest possession both. And now here this horrible man had basically told her she couldn't spell?

In the immortal words of Howard White: how dare he! And as her mouth closed with the clicking sound of her perfect white teeth, in one smooth movement she dumped the precious little tome into her wastepaper basket, and picked up her phone to call the HR department.

If Michael Madison wanted a fight, he got one!

CHAPTER 2

One of the perks of being a cat is that you get to spend so much time with members of the human species. We all know that humans are weird, but they're also weirdly entertaining. In fact I can spend hours watching humans being, well, human. And it was exactly such an opportunity we were having now, watching Tex Poole, our human's dad, engaged in an activity he called 'clearing the attic.'

You have to understand that part of the human experience is to collect junk. Piles and piles of junk. And then at some point, usually in the spring, they suddenly get tired of this pile of junk and start moving it from one place to another. In this case Tex was moving the pile from his attic to the sidewalk, where he hoped other humans would take it away and add it to their own little pile.

It's one of those human pastimes that's simply fascinating for a people watcher like myself, and so I was having a great time watching this particular human now.

"Why is Tex putting all this junk on the sidewalk, Max?"

asked Dooley, who marveled at the sheer volume of stuff the Pooles had amassed in such a small space.

"He hopes other humans will take it away," I said.

"But why did he collect it in the first place?"

"Now that," I said, "is a mystery I still haven't figured out."

I may be an amateur detective, but there are mysteries that are simply too deep to fathom.

Tex had donned an old pair of jeans, an old sweater, and had put a baseball cap on top of his head, as he rooted through the stuff collected in his attic, and it really was a sight to behold, as he opened a box, and either uttered cries of ecstasy, or agony. Ecstasy when he found an old train set he'd played with as a boy, agony when he came upon one of Gran's treasures. Such as there are: 'priceless' artifacts she'd picked up at some garage sale in the year of our Lord 1977. Or the oddly shaped—or oddly misshaped, depending on the eye of the beholder—clay pots that were the product of a pottery class she took in the early eighties.

"Will you look at that?" Tex muttered when he opened yet another old box and took out a tattered little booklet. "I used to read these all the time!"

A glance told me it was a booklet in a series featuring the Hardy Boys.

"Who are the Hardy Boys, Max?" asked Dooley, not missing a beat. "Are they boys that are very hardy?"

"I suppose so," I said. Of course they'd have to be hardy to survive up there in the attic for all these years. At least the attic was dry, but it was also dusty, and not a lot of fun to hang around in for long periods of time.

And so when Tex settled down to read his copy of these hardy Hardy Boys, we decided to take a break from watching him, and go and do the other thing that we enjoy so much: take long naps on any surface we find agreeable. Today I decided to check out the new comforter Chase had brought home with him, and had been extolling the virtues of when he and Odelia put it on the bed that morning.

And as we settled down, I remembered how Chase had said, a catch in his voice, that this would be the first time he and his lady love would get to have first dibs at this nice new thing they got.

How cute humans are. And how naive.

&

While Tex was thus engrossed in the adventures of Frank and Joe Hardy, as chronicled by Franklin W. Dixon, keen eyes had spotted the growing pile of attic surplus on the sidewalk. It just so happened that a troop of girl scouts had selected this particular day to traipse up and down the neighborhood to spread some sweetness and light in the form of girl scout cookies, and so when they turned up on the doorstep of 46 Harrington Street, hoping to extract some coin from the Poole family, their attention was momentarily distracted by the remnants of Tex and Marge Poole's past. So much so that one of their lot, a smallish freckled specimen answering to the name Mabel, felt compelled to pick up a shoebox and take a look inside.

It is, after all, not just cats that marvel at the strange things humans do. Little boys and girls—hardy or not hardy—are just the same. And when Mabel found a stack of letters inside this box, neatly tied together with a red ribbon and a bow, she gibbered excitedly, "You guys, look what I found!"

The other girls of her troop all trooped around, putting their cookie-dispensing mission on hold for the nonce, and gibbered just as excitedly as Mabel extricated the bundle of letters from its receptacle, and gently relieved it from its red ribbon.

"The mailman must have dropped them," said Mabel,

holding the letters reverently. Her daddy was a mailman, and she loved her daddy very much, and had a fervent reverence for the mysterious profession he was engaged in. Handing out presents in the form of letters every day just seemed like such a nice thing to do!

"We have to help the mailman," said a precocious girl with braces named Jackie.

"Jackie is right," a third girl named Frida announced earnestly. "If we don't help the mailman the people these letters are for are going to be very unhappy. My daddy didn't get a letter once and he was so upset he wrote a letter to the post office."

"Your daddy wrote a letter to get a letter?" asked a fourth girl.

Frida nodded, a serious expression on her face. "It was an important letter."

"But how did he know the letter hadn't arrived if it hadn't arrived?" asked a fifth girl, evidencing a keen logic.

This had Jackie stumped for a while, but she quickly rallied. "He must have had a letter telling him he'd get the letter, which is how he knew he didn't get the letter. The second letter, I mean, not the first, which is when he wrote the third letter."

Nods of understanding made the girls' heads bob up and down like a stadium wave, but then Mabel drew their attention to the problem at hand once more.

She was still holding the letters in her grubby little hands. "So what now?" she asked. She'd discovered that the letters were closed, the flaps tucked neatly into their designated opposite flaps, and that there were nice stamps on the letters, and an address written in a sort of spidery scrawl. If she'd been a regular visitor to the doctor, she would have recognized the near-illegible handwriting as typical for your up-and-coming medico. But since her reading skills weren't all that well-developed yet, she had a hard time deciphering the address.

One of the other girls said they all seemed to be addressed to the same street: Harrington Street. And Mabel, whose daddy sometimes talked shop during dinner, said, "This means that all these letters are for people on this street."

"So let's post them," Jackie suggested. "And let's make all the people happy."

The idea warmed Mabel's heart. The notion of an undelivered letter gave this mailman's daughter the pip, and so the mission quickly took on the nature of a sacred assignment. A mission to help all mail-persons the world over.

The next few minutes were spent separating the stack of letters into equal piles, to be divided amongst the members of the troop. It took a while, for there were sixteen letters in all, but only five members, and sixteen doesn't divide by five, so one of the girls was going to have to distribute six letters instead of five. But since Mabel had made this great find, she took it upon herself to carry the extra load.

And it must be said, she did it with gusto. If one good deed promises an uplifted heart and a happy community, imagine what six good deeds will do!

And as Marge Poole idly gazed out of the window, nursing a cup of coffee, and wondering why five girl scouts were rummaging through the pile of attic detritus her husband had placed on the sidewalk, the love letters Tex had written to her more than twenty-five years ago, during a brief but intense courtship, were now on the verge of being redistributed amongst the couple's friends and neighbors.

CHAPTER 3

Popular opinion has it that cats don't enjoy the company of other cats. That we're solitary animals and won't tolerate the kind of intrusion to our peace and quiet other cats—or even dogs—bring. And I have to say that on the whole I don't mind living in a household with three other cats. But sometimes it gets too much. Like today, for instance. I'd just plunged into that pleasant state of drowsiness that is so rewarding, when a sharp voice hauled me out of my slumber.

"Max! What are you doing?"

It was Harriet, entering the bedroom, clearly on the lookout for yours truly.

"I was sleeping," I announced, lazily opening one eye to take in the newcomer.

"How do I look?" she asked, and since I know that Harriet won't take satisfaction from just a cursory glance, I opened my second eye to give her the once-over.

"You look… like you always look," I said, hedging my bets.

"In other words…" she insisted, not letting me off the hook.

"Great!" I said, injecting a modicum of cheerfulness into my voice, inasmuch as one can be cheerful to the person who's just interrupted a perfectly nice nap.

"You could be more specific, Max," she lamented. "Great is so generic."

"Well…" I said, going through my mental thesaurus. "You look, um, amazing?"

But her grimace told me I was wide off the mark. "You, Dooley?" she said.

Dooley, who's often slower than me in the waking-up department, blinked and stared at our friend, not comprehending. "Me Dooley," he said finally. "You Harriet?"

"Oh, for crying out loud!" Harriet said, rolling a pair of very expressive green eyes. "Can I get some constructive criticism here, *por favor*?"

Brutus, who'd also wandered into the room, now said, "You look radiant, sweet pea. Your fur is shinier than the brightest diamond, your eyes are like the twin pools of a crystal mountain lake, and your visage the epitome of loveliness."

Brutus had clearly been reading love poems again. Lately he's taken to browsing websites that cater to the amateur poet, and it showed.

"Oh, sweetie pie," said Harriet, her voice suddenly a purr. "Now *that's* the kind of stuff your budding model likes to hear. You don't think I'm too fat, do you?"

"Not too fat," said Brutus quickly. "Slim like a reed swaying in the breeze."

"Mh," said Harriet. Clearly this particular simile wasn't as apt as the others.

"What's all this about a budding model?" I asked. I might have been napping, but that didn't mean my brain had been fully switched off.

Harriet preened a little. "Guess who's been selected to feature on the cover of next month's *Cat Life*?"

"Fifi?" Dooley suggested, referring to our canine neighbor.

"*CAT Life*, Dooley," Harriet snapped. "Not *Dog Life*."

Dooley thought hard, then finally brightened. "Shanille?"

"No, not Shanille!" Harriet cried. "Me, Dooley, me!"

"You?" asked Dooley, and his surprise was so palpable it took the bloom off the rose of Harriet's excitement, for she directed a dark frown at my friend. Dooley, being Dooley, hardly noticed. "But why you?" he insisted. "You're not a model."

"Well, I'm a model now, so you better get used to it," she said. "And incidentally, you've all been recruited as members of my team."

"And what team is that?" asked Dooley innocently.

"Team Harriet, what else?" she snapped, her patience wearing thin.

"I didn't know you played football," said Dooley, interested.

"Oh, Dooley," Harriet sighed, then turned to me. "I want you to be my spotter, Max."

"Your what?" I asked, stifling a yawn.

"Spotter. You're going to keep a close eye on me and tell me if anything is off."

I stared at her. I could see a lot that was off, but didn't know if it was a good idea to tell her. Her lack of respect for a person's nap time, for one thing.

Brutus, who could see I was struggling with the concept, now piped up, "A person changes from day to day, Max. And the weird thing is that you don't always notice such changes yourself. So it's up to others to draw your attention to them."

"And what changes would this be?" I asked carefully.

"The luster of my coat, for one thing," said Harriet,

holding out a paw. "Or the absence of spots on my nose, for another."

"So Max has to spot your spots?" asked Dooley, trying valiantly to keep up.

"Yes, Dooley," said Harriet with an expressive eyeroll. "Max has to spot my spots."

"And me?" asked Dooley, who seemed to like this new game. "What do you want me to do?"

Harriet gave him a look of such disdain it would have frozen a lesser cat dead on the spot. But not Dooley, who was genuinely excited about the prospect of becoming something big on Team Harriet, whatever it was.

"You can watch my diet," she said after a moment's reflection. "Make sure I don't eat anything fattening, or generally designed to disagree with me."

"So you want me to chew your food for you?" asked Dooley, puzzled.

"Eww, Dooley! I do not want you to chew my food for me! All I'm asking—and if it's too much to ask, just tell me—is that you keep an eye on my caloric intake."

"Your colic..."

"*Caloric.*"

"Um..."

"Just make sure she doesn't eat junk food," Brutus clarified.

Dooley gave me a look of surprise. If ever there was a cat who doesn't allow anyone to come between her and a nice bowl of junk food, it was Harriet. The more additives and colorants and artificial flavoring her wet food contains, the better she likes it. Then again, I guess all cats love the tasty stuff. I know I do. But that doesn't mean I'd attack the person denying it to me with tooth and claw.

"Okay," said Dooley finally, but I could tell that his excitement had waned.

"So Max," said Harriet, "first thing every morning, I want a status report."

"Gotcha," I said.

"And Dooley, you make sure I stick to a healthy and nutritious diet."

"Oh, all right," my friend murmured.

"And me?" asked Brutus. "What do you want me to do, honey blossom?"

Harriet offered her mate a bright smile. "You are my motivation coach, sugar plum. You make sure my energy levels are at an all-time high, all the time. Make sure I'm happy, happy, happy, and keep anything that might upset me away from me. Because we all know that what really matters isn't what's down here," she said, making a circular motion encompassing her face, but what's up here." She tapped her noggin. "It's all about the psychology, baby!"

"Yes, baby!" Brutus echoed, but judging from the look of anguish that I could read in his eyes, his own psychology was in need of a high-energy boost, too!

CHAPTER 4

*H*arriet had finally left, summoning Dooley to join her in the kitchen so they could go over her dietary plan for the next couple of days—until the photoshoot that would immortalize her as a cover model for the iconic magazine *Cat Life*. Brutus turned to me with a distraught sort of look in his eyes. "Tell me the truth, Max. This is pretty much a mission impossible, isn't it?"

"What is?" I asked, fluffing up that nice new comforter. It had to be said: Chase has great taste when it comes to selecting bedding. I liked the man's style.

"Making sure nothing upsets Harriet," he said.

I noticed now for the first time that a gray hair had inserted itself amongst my friend's black fur. Now I know that one gray hair does not an old cat make, but it was a definite sign that being Harriet's mate was wearing my friend out.

I decided not to draw Brutus's attention to the gray hair. And besides, it might simply be something he picked up from lying on the floor. Or even cuddling with his mate, whose fur is as pure and white as the driven snow.

"It is tough to make sure nothing upsets one who's so easily upset," I admitted. "Which is why I don't think you should have accepted the assignment in the first place."

"See? What did I tell you? A mission impossible. Not even Ethan Hunt could keep Harriet happy and energized all the time."

"And nor should you," I pointed out. "It's not your job to keep Harriet happy, Brutus. And besides, happiness is overrated. Cats are simply not designed to be happy all the time. Sometimes we're up and sometimes we're down, and that's just the way it is. Nothing you or me can do about it. Such is life, after all."

"Too true," he said as he jumped up on the bed and had a lie-down.

"And besides, what does it matter if she's happy or sad? As long as she's shining on the day, that's the important thing. And trust me when I tell you that whoever *Cat Life* has on their payroll to take these pictures is going to be someone who knows what they're doing. A cat whisperer, if you will, who can tease the perfect pose out of whatever cat they plunk underneath those bright lights."

My little pep talk didn't miss its effect, for I could see him perk up. "So what do you suggest?"

"I suggest you do exactly what you always do: be a loving partner to Harriet. And I think you'll find that's pretty much all you can do. The rest is up to her."

He sighed contentedly. "When did you become such a clever kitty, Max?"

I shrugged. "Just common sense, I guess. And now let's enjoy this nice new comforter, before the newness wears off."

"Before you leave your orange fluff all over it, you mean."

"Blorange, Brutus," I murmured. "Blorange, not orange."

NIC SAINT

*A*s we all know, the task of clearing out one's attic is a humongous one, which is why most people put it off for as long as there is space to cram just one more item up there. Then, and only then, do they cross off a date on their calendar to venture into this heroic undertaking.

Lucky for Tex, he wasn't alone in having to tackle such an important job. His son-in-law, stalwart cop Chase Kingsley, had kindly volunteered to give him a helping hand. The fact that Marge had told Odelia to tell Chase to pitch in was neither here nor there, and not an aspect of the matter Chase had bothered to mention to his father-in-law.

And so it was that both men lugged old carpets down the stairs, an ancient roll-top desk that had belonged to Vesta's grandfather, and even a couple of bulky typewriters that dated back to the time when Tex's grandad had had ambitions to become the next Harold Robbins, back when Mr. Robbins was still the *ne plus ultra* of bestselling authors.

All this routing around a dusty old attic and carrying stuff here and there makes a person thirsty, and so in between all this physical activity, they took regular breaks in the kitchen, to sip down some cooling lemonade.

"Dad?" asked Chase as he first wiped his brow then his lips. "Can I ask you a personal question?"

"Shoot, son," said Tex. Once upon a time he had shivered violently when being addressed by this young whippersnapper as 'Dad,' but the fever had long since passed. Nowadays he enjoyed having a son, and not having had to pay for his upbringing, or struggle through those awful teenage years, when boys grow a mullet or a mohawk, and announce they want to be the next Bieber or Dave Grohl.

"How did you ever become such a great dad, Dad?"

Tex, who'd been in the process of biting down on an

apple, paused and adopted a weary look. Parental advice. Always a tough proposition.

"I mean, now that I have a kid of my own, I find myself wondering what constitutes a great dad, you know? And I know you did such a great job with Odelia, that I'll bet you've got some amazing tips to share with a new dad like me."

Tex nodded, chewing his apple meditatively, and stalling for time.

"Because to be honest? Half the time I haven't got a clue what I'm doing."

Nor did Tex, but he wasn't going to admit that and fall off the pedestal Chase had just put him on. Since people rarely put him on a pedestal, he quite enjoyed the experience. "Well…" he said. "First off, thanks for calling me a great dad."

"Well, you obviously are," said Chase. "Just look at Odelia, and what a wonderful person she turned out to be."

"Odelia is a wonderful person, that's true," said Tex.

"She's the best."

"Like you say, she's the best."

"So what's the secret, Dad? What's the secret to being a good dad?"

"I'll tell you what the secret is," said Tex finally, having given the matter some thought—the first time in his life he had, in fact. "It's being a role model, son."

"Uh-huh. Makes sense."

"Setting a good example."

"Okay."

"And most importantly: by always being positive and upbeat." He wagged a finger in his son-in-law's face. "Never let them see you sad, kid. That's the secret."

"Never let them see you sad," Chase repeated, clearly in awe of these wise words. "I like it, Dad. I really do. Never let them see you sad. Simple but brilliant."

He clapped the kid on the back. "You know, I could talk

hours about what makes the perfect dad—a dad like me, I mean—but we've got an attic to clean out, and daylight is waning, son. So let's get back to it, shall we?"

"Sure thing," said Chase, but it was obvious he was still mulling over Tex's words, those pearls of wisdom the doctor had casually dispensed to his Padawan.

It touched Tex's heart. A wise man passing on his wisdom to his young son. How wonderful. How moving. Now if only he knew what he was talking about.

CHAPTER 5

Vesta Muffin and Scarlett Canyon were hard at work in the offices of the *Hampton Cove Gazette*, where editor-in-chief Dan Goory had given them their own desk. The two ladies wrote the Dear Gabi column for the *Gazette*, which had become quite a hit with readers, and was, according to the SEO boffin Dan had once hired to overhaul the website, one of the most-read, best-rated items on the site.

"What a pile," Vesta sighed as she leaned back. Along with the growing success of their column, the number of letters and emails had also exploded, and it wasn't unusual to get dozens of them every single day. Up to them the task of selecting those few nuggets that would be of interest to the *Gazette's* wider readership.

"Now this is odd," said Scarlett as she frowned at her screen.

"What is?"

"Three different emails from three different people, but all of them from the same company. At least I think they're from the same company. Their email addresses all end with 'advantagepublishing.com.'" She looked up. "Advantage Publishing is the company that publishes—"

"*Glimmer*," said Vesta, her interest piqued. *Glimmer* was only one of the most popular women's magazines in the country. Right up there with *Good Housekeeping*, *Vogue* and *Cosmopolitan*. "So what are they saying?"

"Well, the first one is from a Natalie Ferrara. She says she's pregnant with her boss's baby, only her boss doesn't want the baby. In fact he told her to get an abortion, and not only that, but he broke up with her and now she's on her own."

"What a jerk."

Scarlett nodded. "She says she can't stop crying, and doesn't know what to do."

"She still works for the guy who knocked her up and then dumped her?"

"The email doesn't say," said Scarlett. "But I suppose so."

"If I could just lay my hands on the guy..."

"And then there's Tom Mitchell. He says he's been in love with one of his colleagues for years, but she doesn't even know he exists. He wants to know how to get out of the friend zone."

"If she doesn't know he exists, he's not even in the friend zone," Vesta commented. "More like the nothing zone."

"And finally we have Doris Booth, whose boss just gave her a copy of *Elements of Style*, by Strunk and White, basically telling her she can't spell." She looked up. "Doris works as a publicist, so language is supposed to be her special skill. Her forte. I think it's safe to say she's pretty upset about the whole business."

"I can imagine," Vesta murmured. "What's going on at Advantage? Three people write us on the same day. A pregnant woman dumped by her boss, a guy hopelessly in love with a colleague, and a woman being insulted by her boss."

"Pity we don't know more," said Scarlett as she scanned through the first email once again. It had clearly touched a chord. "Tough to give advice. I mean, what can you tell these people?"

"Not a lot," Vesta agreed.

"What are the rules on Gabi getting in touch with these people and teasing some more information out of them?"

"I don't think it's the done thing."

"No, I didn't think so either."

They both pondered the issue for a moment, then Vesta's eyes brightened. "I just had a great idea," she announced, sitting up a little straighter.

"Uh-oh."

"Why don't you and me take the Gabi show on the road?"

"What do you mean?"

"I think we both agree that it's hard to give advice when you don't have enough information, right?"

"Right."

"So why don't we get the information we need the old-fashioned way?" And when Scarlett simply stared at her, not comprehending, she added, "We apply for a job at Advantage Publishing, get to know this trio of letter writers, and then we can tailor our advice to their needs!"

Scarlett's frown indicated she wasn't as excited as she could have been. Her next words confirmed this. "I think you're nuts."

"No, but it's brilliant! We apply for a job, get hired, and that way we can look around, see for ourselves what's going on, and give the kind of advice these people need and deserve."

"And how are we going to get hired? We're both senior citizens. And if you hadn't noticed, job offers for our age bracket are pretty much non-existent."

"We'll do it like in that Nancy Meyers movie."

"*The Holiday*? We switch places with some ditzy rich blonde?"

"No, the one with Robert De Niro and Anne Hathaway, where she hires him as her senior intern." She spread her arms. "We'll be senior interns at *Glimmer*! How cool is that!"

Scarlett's initial reluctance to recognize the brilliance of her plan slightly melted. "That would be cool," she admitted. "But how do you know this senior internship isn't something that only exists in a Nancy Meyers movie?"

"Oh, who cares? If it doesn't exist, it should exist, and if they won't accept us, we'll simply accuse them of ageism, and threaten to sue. And if that doesn't work, we can always ask Dan to get in touch with whatever bozo is in charge of Advantage and put in a good word for us."

"Mh," said Scarlett, but Vesta could see she was warming to her idea. "I've always wanted to see what a company like Advantage looks like on the inside," she said.

"And now you'll get the chance." She spread her arms. "We're going to help out three people, Scarlett. Three unhappy souls. Now what can be more gratifying? And if we pull this off, we could make it a regular thing: drop in on the people writing us, and get some background information before writing up a column."

"It almost sounds too good to be true," said Scarlett wistfully, as she gave her friend a look of suspicion. "What's the catch? Cause there has to be a catch, right?"

"No catch," she assured her friend. "We're simply going to spread some sweetness and light. Just like we always do. Only now we'll do it as Dear Gabi!"

CHAPTER 6

Marge Poole had just placed a copy of the latest bestseller—*Heart of a Turtle Dove*—on the rack when a light cough made her jump. She clutched a hand to her heart. "You startled me," she told Mrs. Samson, her oldest and best customer.

The elderly lady was holding a letter in her hand, and had a sort of feverish look in her eye. The same look she got when she was the first to snatch up a particularly spicy new novel that had just been added to the library's collection.

"What have you got there?" asked Marge.

"It was in my mailbox just now," said Mrs. Samson. "Even though it's addressed to you. I hope you don't mind, but I read it before I realized it wasn't for me."

"Addressed to me?" asked Marge with a frown as she accepted the letter from Mrs. Samson's hand. "Who could have sent me a—" But then she recognized the handwriting. It was Tex's. She quickly took out the letter and scanned it. Her heart sank like a stone. "But this is…" It was an old letter. One Tex had written when they first met in college. Back when his writing was still more or less readable, before medical school had its full effect, intent as it is on teaching young doctors how to stop writing in a legible way and adopt some obscure scrawl.

"It's pretty spicy," Mrs. Samson commented. "I especially like the way he compares certain parts of your anatomy to a peach. A ripe peach," she added for good measure. Her eyes were shiny and very, very bright.

Color crept up Marge's cheeks, and she felt her face and neck burn. "But how did—how could—where did this…" And then she remembered. Tex was clearing out the attic. He must have found a box of these old letters and… An image flashed before her mind's eye of a troop of girl scouts gathered around the pile of stuff her husband had put out on the sidewalk. And more in particular a box of… letters! "God, no," she groaned, closing her eyes in abject dismay. "Tell me he didn't…"

"Looks like your husband wants the whole world to know how he feels about you," said Mrs. Samson. "The hot stud."

"Yes, well, these letters weren't meant for the whole world to see."

"There's more?" asked Mrs. Samson, not hiding her excitement. "Can I read them?"

"These are my private letters, Margaret," Marge explained. "They were never meant to be seen by anyone other than myself and my husband."

"He's got mad skillz, your husband," commented the old lady. "This stuff is hotter than *Fifty Shades of Grey*. Are you sure his name isn't Christian Grey?"

"Yes, I'm quite sure," she said as she tucked the letter into the envelope again. She then placed a hand on Mrs. Samson's shoulder. "Would you mind watching the library for half an hour, Margaret?"

"Oh, sure." The old lady gave her a shrewd look. "On one condition."

"Name it."

"Give me another one of your husband's hot letters to read? They're so good."

She grimaced. "I'll see what I can do."

She grabbed her phone, dumped it into her purse, hiked the latter up her shoulder, and was off on a light trot out the door.

She was a woman on a mission now: to retrieve as many letters as she could before the whole street got a collective heart attack and branded her with a scarlet letter!

As she hurried home, the first person she saw was Marcie Trapper. Her next-door neighbor was standing next to the mailbox, reading a letter, her cheeks flushed and her face contorted into a sort of crazy grimace. Before Marge could duck out of sight, Marcie looked up, and the two women's eyes locked.

And as a grin slowly crept up Marcie's face, Marge felt her legs go a little wobbly. She tried to remember what Tex had written in those letters of his, but it was such a long time ago—more than twenty-five years—that she simply couldn't. If Mrs. Samson's letter was anything to go by, though, it was pretty hot stuff!

"Now why is Tex sending me a letter postmarked twenty-seven years ago?" asked Marcie. "And full of some pretty sexy stuff? Is he having a MeToo moment?"

"No, he is not. If you look closely, you'll see that the letter is actually not addressed to you, Marcie," said Marge, trying to keep her cool, which under the circumstances was a tough proposition. "That letter was addressed to me, and was accidentally posted in your mailbox this morning."

Marcie frowned at the letter. "Oh, I see," she said with a

touch of disappointment. "Marcie or Marge. It's almost the same thing."

"So can I have it back, please?" asked Marge, holding out her hand.

"Just a moment," said Marcie, yanking the letter out of her reach. "When Tex writes, 'I want to put my hot hands on your juicy, ripe—'"

"Yes, yes, yes!" said Marge. "I know what he wrote." Even though she didn't.

"He should have been a writer," said Marcie. "He's got the talent, you know."

"Yes, I know," said Marge. "Now can I have my letter back, please?"

Reluctantly, Marcie placed the letter in her hand. "But why did he post it in my mailbox, is what I would like to know. And I'm sure Ted would like to know, too."

"Tex didn't post it."

"Oh, so you did?" asked Marcie, clutching a hand to her chest to gather her dress around herself, just in case Marge tried any funny business.

"No! Of course not!"

Marcie seemed hurt by this comment. "Nothing is impossible, you know. I mean, we have been neighbors for a long time, and I like to consider you a friend. And sometimes, between friends… feelings will develop. Feelings that are…" But when Marge just stared at her, she quickly collected herself. "Forget what I said."

"Tex is clearing out the attic," Marge said.

"You don't have to explain yourself to me, Marge," said Marcie, a little snippy.

"He must have accidentally put a box of these old letters outside, where a troop of girl scouts found it, and started distributing them along the street."

"A troop of girl scouts did drop by earlier," said Marcie,

nodding. "I bought cookies from them. Very expensive they were, too. And not very tasty either." Then she brightened. "Oh, I see what must have happened. They probably thought Bambi Wiggins accidentally dropped these while doing her rounds, and decided to give her a helping hand by putting them in their designated mailboxes."

"Exactly," said Marge, glad to have finally gotten the message across.

"Ted never wrote letters like that to me," said Marcie, and there was a touch of disappointment in her voice. "You're a lucky lady, Marge Poole."

"I know," said Marge. Though truth be told, she didn't feel very lucky, knowing that perhaps a dozen more of her neighbors were reading her private letters at that exact moment, and probably wondering whether to file a MeToo complaint against Tex!

༄

Hampton Cove's Christian Grey wannabe, meanwhile, was at work in his office, patiently listening to Ida Baumgartner, who was claiming against better advice that the red bump on her arm was skin cancer, and demanding that Tex launch a full investigation into the suspicious bump before it was too late!

And as Tex took a closer look at the offending bump, which was clearly a simple mole, and had no ambition, nor had it ever had the ambition, to be anything other than a simple mole, suddenly Ida took a letter out of her purse and started reading in a loud declamatory voice, "I want you. I've never wanted a woman more than I want you. I think about you day and night, and my dreams are even hotter than my thoughts. Oh, to feel your lips on my lips. To feel your burning body against mine! I count the days until we meet again... Marge!"

Tex, who'd been listening with mild interest, jerked up at the mention of his wife's name. In fact he jerked so hard he felt a sudden twinge in his back and exclaimed, "Ouch!"

"Ouch, indeed!" Ida snapped. The older lady sat eyeing him with a disapproving eye, clutching her purse in her lap. "What's the meaning of delivering a letter of such clearly *pornographic* nature in my mailbox, Doctor Poole?"

"But, but, but..." Tex stuttered.

"I found this piece of filth just before I set out for our appointment. At first I thought it must be some kind of joke, but then of course I recognized your handwriting, which is very distinctive. If you want to make advances, young man, I must warn you that I don't take kindly to this kind of unwanted attention!"

"But, but, but!"

"In fact I had a good mind to take this letter to the police, and file a complaint against you for sexual harassment!"

"But, but, but!!!"

Ida's face softened. "But then I saw the date on the letter, which is dated twenty-seven years ago. And obviously since my name isn't Marge, but your wife's is, it soon became clear to me there must have been some terrible mistake. Either that, or you have gone completely mad!"

"But how did—I mean, where did... How could this..." He took the letter from his patient's hands and studied it. And then it hit him. The attic! His cheeks flamed even as his Adam's apple performed a series of light somersaults in his throat. He must have accidentally put out a box of his letters, and somehow some prankster must have thought it funny to put them in mailboxes all across the neighborhood. "Oh, God," he muttered, and groaned freely. And so he quickly proceeded to put Ida in possession of the sordid facts pertaining to the case.

Ida, who, in spite of her many ailments, was a tough cookie, showed that she also had a heart. She patted him lightly on the knee. "No need to be alarmed, Tex. It happens to the best of us. But mind that you don't do it again, you hear? Not everyone is as liberal-minded as I am. Some people out there might take offense."

He informed Ida that the suspicious spot was not suspicious at all, but all the while his mind was spinning out of control. How many letters were there? And how many neighbors had received them? Dozens? Hundreds? He remembered he'd been very active back in the day when he was courting Marge, the loveliest girl he'd ever met, and today still the most wonderful woman he'd ever known.

She'd be furious if she found out. Mad as a wet hen, in fact. And rightly so!

CHAPTER 7

Margaret Samson, left alone to run the library in Marge's absence, enjoyed the privilege of being able to stamp people's library cards and give them reading advice in the process. An avid reader herself, she knew her way around the library, which was like her home away from home, its librarian a personal friend.

So when a man walked up to her, asking if she could give him some tips on what to put on his To Be Read pile, she kindly asked what type of book he favored.

"Oh, anything that adds a little spice to my life will do," he said with a grin.

He was a handsome man, with a full crop of dark hair, graying at the temples, which gave him the distinguished look of a surgeon on *Grey's Anatomy*, while at the same time sporting the build of a lifeguard. He was casually dressed in jeans and a sweater, and had one of those strong jawlines she liked so much in a man.

"I think I've got just the ticket for you, young man," she said, as she reached for her phone and pulled up the letter

Tex had written to his wife. "Now tell me if this isn't spicy," she said as she handed him the phone.

He scanned the letter, and much to her satisfaction almost immediately quirked an eyebrow. "Hot stuff," he said appreciatively. "Who wrote this, you?"

"Nah," she said. "You know Marge Poole? The librarian?"

"I've seen her around," said the man. "Blond? Willowy?"

"Yeah, I'd describe her as willowy," said Margaret as she eyed the man closely. "Why? She your type, Mr…"

"Rapp," said the guy. "Gary Rapp. She could be my type," he said. "But I thought she was married to some doctor?"

"Not for long, she won't be," said Margaret with a low chuckle.

"Trouble in paradise, huh?"

"Isn't there always?" She might love a good Happy Ever After in the romance novels she read on a daily basis, but she was no fool. No woman likes it when her husband of twenty-five years puts the love letters he once sent out for trash collection. That's just wrong. And besides, Tex had always struck her as an idiot.

Just then, the lady under discussion walked in, a harried look on her face.

"Hey, Marge," said Margaret. "I want you to meet Gary. Gary, meet Marge."

"Hey, there, Marge," said Gary, putting that unctuous spin in his voice only the best ones can. "Margaret was just telling me what a great librarian you are."

"She was? Why, thanks, Margaret."

"Did you get your letters back?" asked Margaret, darting a quick look to Gary to see how he would respond. The man's eyes lit up at the memory of that letter. Clearly his interest was piqued. Oh, how she loved to play matchmaker!

"Not yet," said Marge. "But I'm going to."

"Marge's husband put his love letters in the trash,"

Margaret explained, and watched Marge wince. "Now I'm asking you, what kind of a husband does that?"

"I'm sure it was just an innocent mistake," said Marge, as her eyes flicked to Gary and away again.

"If a woman wrote me a letter like that, I'd treasure it for the rest of my life," Gary assured them.

"It wasn't actually me who wrote it," said Marge.

"Oh?"

"See, Tex wrote the letters and I wrote him back, and I put the ones he sent me in a box and kept them, while he managed to lose the ones I wrote him."

Margaret shook her head and tsk-tsked freely. "Lost them. How about that?"

"I hope you get them all back," said Gary. "It's terrible when you lose a personal memento like that. Especially through no fault of your own."

"Yeah, it's not a pleasant experience," said Marge. "But let's not dwell on it."

"No, let's not," Gary agreed.

"Gary likes to read spicy novels," said Margaret, sensing that the conversation might come to a standstill. "Exactly my kind of novel, in other words."

"Oh, you read romance?" asked Marge.

"Yeah, I do," said Gary, giving her a half-smile. "Unusual for a guy, I know."

"Oh, no. You'd be surprised how many men actually read romance."

"You're kidding. Really?"

"Really. So you're not alone, Gary."

"Maybe you could show Gary around the library?" Margaret goaded. "He's in search of some fresh reading material, and no one gives better advice than you."

"Of course. Absolutely," said Marge, always ready to assist a customer.

And as they went off, chatting amiably amongst themselves, Margaret nodded knowingly to herself. The first hurdle a couple must take had been successfully taken. The part where they meet for the first time and feel that spark. And that a spark had been felt was a certainty for this old hand at the romance game.

Tex Poole would rue the day he put those letters in the trash!

※

One of the perks of being a reporter is that you don't have to punch in at nine o'clock or out at five. And since Odelia's husband was a detective and he, too, could be flexible with his work schedule, the couple now stood in the entrance hall of the daycare center where they had just dropped off Grace.

Fortunately for them, their little girl was a sociable and happy child, who loved nothing better than to make new friends. And as they waved goodbye to their darling sweetheart, Grace didn't even give them the time of day, engrossed as she was in a deep conversation with a friend, mommy and daddy already forgotten.

What the two toddlers were saying to each other, exactly, was a mystery to anyone, as it amounted to nothing more than disjointed sounds and nonsense words. But apparently, and in their very own way, they managed to communicate.

"I hate to leave her here," said Odelia, who only now noticed how her husband had a big smile on his face. So big, in fact, that he looked a little ridiculous.

"We can't always ask your gran to babysit, babe," said Chase. "Or your mom and dad. They have their own stuff to do."

"Yeah, I know. But still."

He placed an arm around her shoulders. "And look at the bright side: they say that kids who go to daycare and learn to socialize end up doing a lot better in school and also in life."

"I guess," she said. But she still missed her baby girl. If possible, she would take her along everywhere she went, but she knew that simply wasn't possible.

"Cheer up, babe!" said Chase, that rictus grin apparently a fixture on his face. "Grace is healthy, happy and she's got a great future ahead of her and so have we!"

She frowned at her hubby. "Is everything all right with you, babe?"

"Of course! Everything is great! Everything is amazing! Wonderful!"

"Easy there, tiger. You're starting to sound like Tony Robbins there."

"Oh, wow. What a compliment. What a great thing to say! You're making me so happy right now!" And he actually gave her two thumbs up to go with the crazy smile.

She shook her head, but decided not to pry. If she didn't know any better, she would have thought he was high on some illegal substance, but she knew Chase wasn't into drugs. He didn't even smoke or drink. Most likely he was trying to make her feel better about leaving Grace at the daycare center. Which was so sweet of him.

"It'll be fine," she said, glancing back at their little girl one last time. She said it as much to Chase as to herself, trying to drown out the little voice that told her she was a bad mother for putting her kid in daycare. "It'll be just fine."

CHAPTER 8

When you've lived in the Poole household for as long as I have, you come to expect the unexpected at every turn of your existence. And let me tell you: a quiet existence it is not!

Take today, for instance. When I woke up at the foot of Odelia and Chase's bed that morning, little did I know that it wouldn't be a day like other days. Oh, sure, it started out that way, with Grace letting all and sundry know that she was awake and expecting to be fed posthaste, and Chase and Odelia occupying the bathroom to get themselves ready to face another day.

"Why don't humans simply lick themselves clean, Max?" asked Dooley when Odelia came hurrying out of the bathroom, her wet hair wrapped in a towel on top of her head, and went in search of some necessary undergarments.

"I don't think they're quite limber enough to reach every part of their anatomy," I said, having given this matter some serious thought in the past. "And also, they don't have the patience to apply their tongues to so much acreage."

Humans are busy people, you see, always rushing off

somewhere and trying to squeeze as much activity into every single minute of every single day as humanly possible. They lack the patience to spend hours grooming themselves, like cats do.

Ordinarily Dooley and I ride with Odelia to work and spend the day in her office, or out and about interviewing people, and sometimes even solving the odd mystery. Today was going to be different, though, as Odelia explained to us once Grace had been fed and dressed and ready to go to the daycare center.

"I have an important matter to discuss with you guys," she announced, taking a seat on the bed next to us.

"You're not going to get a divorce, are you?" Dooley asked anxiously.

"Now why would I get a divorce?" said Odelia with a puzzled smile.

"Because Chase accidentally sent your love letters to all the neighbors, and now you're madder than a wet hen and you're not going to speak to him again?"

There had been a slight contretemps in the Poole household, when Tex had put his old love letters to his wife out for trash collection. Instead of a trashman, though, a troop of girl scouts had discovered the letters, and now the entire neighborhood was privy to Tex's private thoughts in re his erstwhile affections toward his future wife. Suffice it to say Marge was not amused.

"Writing letters is not exactly the done thing anymore, Dooley," said Odelia. "In fact Chase never wrote me any love letters at all. Whatever he had to say to me, he said in person."

What she didn't mention was that Chase is not exactly the type of person who carries his heart on his sleeve. Or writes love letters. So when I picture their courtship, I can't imagine it consisted of more than a few lusty looks and grunts of appreciation from Chase's side. We may be living in the age of the modern man, who cries when he cuts himself peeling a potato, but Chase is more akin to the man of yore, back when men were men and the dinosaurs still walked the earth.

"Okay, so Gran has asked me to loan you to her for an important mission and after careful consideration I've decided to say yes." She paused, so we could absorb this message, then continued, "The mission has to do with her Dear Gabi column, and you'll act as her eyes and ears throughout. Think you can do that?"

"Oh, absolutely," I said, and would have asked her about a million questions about this 'important mission,' but unfortunately this was all the time she had.

"Gran will pick you up around... now," she said, checking her watch, and just as she spoke these words, Gran's voice sounded from downstairs.

"Are you guys ready!" the old lady bellowed. "Cause I am!"

And so our unusual adventure began. Why Gran hadn't selected Harriet and Brutus to assist her in this important task was beyond me. Perhaps she felt that Harriet was so busy getting ready for her photoshoot that she wouldn't be able to focus on the job at hand. Whatever the reason, moments later we were riding in the car with Gran and Scarlett, and our destination was: Advantage Publishing.

"We've been selected as Advantage Publishing's first-ever senior interns," Scarlett announced proudly. "It's going to be a blast!"

"How much are they paying you?" asked Dooley.

"They're not paying us anything," said Gran. "We're interns, and interns work for free."

"We do get a free subscription to *Glimmer*," said Scarlett. "And free coffee."

"So you're going to work for these people and not get

paid?" I asked, trying to get to the bottom of this strange conceit.

"We're doing this for the good of our readers," said Gran. "Giving something back to our loyal audience."

"And also, Dan is paying us for our time," said Scarlett.

"Yeah, there's that," Gran admitted.

Advantage Publishing was housed in a new building in a semi-industrial zone that houses many such buildings and companies. It all looked very snazzy and ultra-modern, just as you would expect from the publisher of *Glimmer* and *Glitter*, but also of *Fish & Tackle*, the amateur fisherman's friend, and of course *Cat Life*, coincidentally the magazine that had selected Harriet as its cover model.

Upon arrival, Gran and Scarlett received a pair of neat badges, but when it came time to announce myself and Dooley, it appeared some wires had gotten crossed. The receptionist stared down at us, then up at Gran, then stared at us some more. "But... pets are not allowed in the building," she explained.

"These are not pets," said Gran. "These are emotional support animals."

"Yeah, we need them," said Scarlett. "For emotional support," she added.

"You wouldn't take a blind person's guide dog away from them, would you?" said Gran. "We need these cats. Without them we won't be able to function."

"Oh-kay," said the girl, then took her phone and walked away for a few moments, busily talking into her phone, and presumably asking advice from one of her higher-ups. When she returned, she had a big smile on her face. "It's all right, Mrs. Muffin. You can bring your emotional support animals into the building now." She then gave me a pointed look. "They are... potty trained, aren't they?"

"Of course," said Gran. "Max and Dooley are highly-trained professionals."

"What have we been trained at, Max?" asked Dooley as we proceeded to the bank of elevators.

"Didn't you hear? Going to the potty," I said, as we hurried to keep up with Gran and Scarlett.

"I just hope they have a potty to go to," he said, panting a little.

It was a big building, all concrete and glass, with many floors and plenty of people occupying those floors, all busy working on their respective computers. Soon enough, though, we found our desks—or at least Gran and Scarlett found their desks, with Dooley and myself being relegated to a corner of said desks.

Then again, if you're going to be an emotional support animal, which we now apparently were, you have to learn to take these little setbacks in stride.

"So what is our mission?" I asked once Gran had placed a minor potted plant on top of her desk—her way of staking her claim, I guess.

"Our mission is twofold," said Gran as she started wrestling with her office chair, putting it higher, then lower, then adjusting the tilt of the backrest, then cursing loudly while she pulled levers and yanked and turned and kicked at the plethora of knobs the thing contained. "Do you see that woman over there?"

I scanned the horizon, and located the woman she referred to. "The pretty blond one?" I asked.

"Bingo. Her name is Natalie Ferrara and she's pregnant."

"Good for her," I said, nodding. "Who's the baby daddy?"

"That's the problem," she said. "Her boss is the baby daddy, but the moment she told him about the baby, he said he didn't want to be the daddy. In other words, he dumped her, and now he wants her to get an abortion."

"Ouch."

"And so Natalie is very upset and wrote to Gabi asking her for advice. Which is why we're here. To assess the situation and figure out how to proceed. The second part of our mission is that guy over there. His name is Tom Mitchell and he's in love with a colleague who doesn't give him the time of day. So we need to figure out who this colleague is, and if we can bring them together somehow."

"Tough mission," I said. These Cupid missions are always difficult to pull off.

"And there's a third person," said Gran, pushing her glasses further up her nose as she searched around. "But I don't see her right now. Maybe she quit. Her boss gifted her a copy of the *Elements of Style*, which she took to mean he doesn't think she can spell. Her name is Doris Booth and this is what she looks like."

She showed us a picture on her phone, then flicked through to pictures of Natalie Ferrara and Tom Mitchell, which she had obviously found on the internet.

"So I want you guys to hang around, discreetly listen in on conversations, and then report back to me with any office gossip relevant to our three targets. Is that understood?"

"Absolutely," I said. Now that I had a deeper understanding of our mission, I was feeling more relaxed. It seemed like something we might be able to pull off.

"Now if I can only get this stupid chair to behave," she grumbled annoyedly.

CHAPTER 9

It was an interesting experience for me to be part of a large office like this. I had been in office settings before, of course, but Odelia's office is a small one, only occupied by herself and her boss Dan Goory. And then there's Chase, who has several colleagues. But Advantage Publishing was clearly one step up from the police station, scale-wise, I mean. Gran had cleared a portion of her desk, and now Dooley and I had a nice overview of the office from our new vantage point.

"This place is big, Max," Dooley marveled. "I've never seen so many people working together before. What do they all do all day? And why are they so busy?"

"Publishing several magazines is a lot of work, Dooley," I said. "All those pages have to be filled with copy and pictures, and then those pictures and articles have to be put in the right place so you're going to need editors and layout people."

"Odelia could work here," said my friend. "It would be like a promotion."

"I think Odelia likes the freedom she has working for the

Gazette. In a corporate environment like this you always have some boss to answer to."

We glanced in the direction of a glass cubicle in the corner of the large office space, where Michael Madison ruled his empire with an iron fist, according to Gran. We could see him seated behind his desk now, talking to Natalie. When she left his office, she looked both sad and upset, and Michael Madison looked angry.

"I think they had a fight about the baby," said Dooley.

"Yeah, I think so, too," I agreed.

"Poor Natalie. Pregnant and unloved."

"She may be pregnant, but she's not unloved," I said, and gestured to Tom Mitchell, who sat eyeing Natalie fervently, with a sort of puppy dog look on his face. "It wouldn't surprise me if Natalie is the colleague Tom is secretly in love with," I announced.

Gran had noticed the same thing, and whispered, "I think you just might be right, Max! Which would make our job a whole lot easier!"

"How do you mean?" asked Dooley.

"If we can get those two together, it would solve two problems in one go!"

"Quiet, you guys," said Scarlett. "Someone's coming!"

And indeed there was. A young man with a floppy hairdo was heading in our direction. He was pushing a cart loaded with items that looked like mail. When he finally reached us, he gave us a curious glance, before addressing Gran.

"Vesta Muffin and Scarlett Canyon?" he asked.

"That's us," said Gran.

"You've got mail," said the kid with a grin, and dropped an envelope on Gran's desk. "Contracts, probably," he explained. "Just sign them and drop them off with me. I'll make sure they get where they're supposed to be. I'm Danny, by the way. I work in the mailroom."

"Yeah, I thought as much," said Gran.

"You guys are part of this new senior intern program, aren't you?"

"Yep, that's us," said Scarlett.

"You don't look senior to me," said Danny, as he gave Scarlett an appreciative look. "How old are you? Forty? Fifty?"

Scarlett giggled. "Hasn't anyone ever told you? A lady never tells and a gentleman never asks."

"Then I guess I shouldn't have asked."

"I won't tell if you won't," said Scarlett, batting her eyelashes at the kid.

She was dressed to impress on her first day on the job. For the occasion she was wearing an actual business suit, which made her look more like a high-powered executive than an intern. In fact she looked as if she owned the place.

"Scarlett is my age," said Gran, dropping a bucket of ice water on this budding office romance. Danny stared at her for a moment, then at Scarlett, and finally shook his head. "That's impossible. You look at least twenty years younger."

"Why, thank you, Danny," said Scarlett.

Gran, who was grinding her dentures, now growled, "Don't you have places to be, sonny boy? People to see?"

"Hold your horses, granny," said Danny, then directed a wink at Scarlett and was off to deliver more mail.

"Twenty years younger, my ass," Gran growled.

"Now let's not forget why we're here, Vesta," said Scarlett. "And befriending the mailroom boy may work in our favor. Guys like Danny know everyone and everything about a place like this."

"You're right," Gran reluctantly admitted. "Go on. Seduce him if you must."

"I'm not going to seduce a kid like that—are you crazy!"

Then she sighed. "He is yummy, though, isn't he? How old do you think he is? Twenty? Twenty-five?"

"More like fifteen."

"Oh, nonsense. If he's old enough to work here, he's old enough to…"

"Let's not forget why we're here, Scarlett," Gran admonished her friend.

"Touché," said Scarlett with a grin. "So how do you want to work this?"

But before they could decide on a strategy of campaign, a young woman joined us. She was the office manager, and was there to teach Gran and Scarlett the ropes. Turns out they'd been hired to assist the office staff in some minor and less appealing tasks. Such as there are: updating customer lists, checking addresses, correcting listings for the accounting department… All in all, not exactly the most exciting work! But Gran and Scarlett set themselves to it with gusto.

"And what are we supposed to do?" asked Dooley, once the office manager had left.

"We're going to do what we do best," I said. "Which is to snoop around!"

And so we hopped down from the desk, and made our way over to Natalie's desk, which was closest to the big boss.

As we approached, we drew a lot of attention from the office staff, who had presumably never seen a pair of cats before. But since word had spread that the two new interns had brought along their emotional support animals, at least no one tried to evict us.

We took up position next to the window, which coincidentally put us within hearing distance of Natalie Ferrara, hoping to glean some information that would make Gran and Scarlett's task a little easier.

"She seems sad, Max," said Dooley.

And she did. So sad, in fact, that I could detect at least fifteen Kleenexes in her wastepaper basket. She was talking into her phone when we arrived, keeping the volume low so no one else could hear.

"The least you can do is cook dinner, Luke. No, we're not going to order out again tonight. Do you know how much this is costing me?" She listened for a moment, then closed her eyes and shook her head. "Just… do it, all right?" And then she hung up, stared before her for a few moments, and got back to work.

"Boyfriend trouble?" Dooley suggested.

"Could be," I said. "Though I doubt it. She's obviously still crazy about her boss, otherwise she wouldn't be crying her eyes out all day."

"Poor girl," said Dooley. "Her boss doesn't deserve her."

But since there was nothing more to learn here, we moved on to Gran and Scarlett's second target. Tom was also tapping away at his computer, but as we settled in next to his desk, the same mailroom kid arrived, looked left and right, and lowered his voice as he addressed the bespectacled young man.

"Guess what," he said. "Natalie is pregnant."

"What?" said Tom, clearly taken aback by this piece of news.

"I've got it from a reliable source," announced Danny. "And guess who the father is."

"I have no idea," said Tom, frowning darkly at this bearer of bad news.

"None other than Mad Madison himself!"

Tom almost fell from his chair, but recovered quickly. "You're crazy."

"No, it's true! Susan from accounting was in Madison's office this morning, and caught the last snatches of a phone call. Something about an abortion. And when she checked closer, turns out he was talking to Natalie."

"So? She's his PA. He could have been talking about anyone. Or asking her to check something for research purposes. No reason to assume she's having his baby."

"That's what I said. But listen to this. Couple of days ago Susan saw a bill from some posh hotel in town. Room booked for two in Madison's name. So just out of curiosity she called the hotel to double-check, and they told her Madison took that room, all right. Him and some young babe. Blond and blue-eyed." He arched a meaningful eyebrow. "Remind you of someone? Oh, and also, it wasn't the first time either. Turns out they've been having regular dates in that same hotel for the past couple of months. And when I passed Natalie's desk yesterday, I saw a card for some abortion clinic on her desk with Madison's handwriting on it. It said, 'My treat! Just do it!!!' When Natalie saw me checking it out, she quickly covered the card with a copy of *Glimmer*. But I know what I saw, buddy. Your girl is having an affair with the big chief—and got herself knocked up in the process!"

"She's not my girl," said Tom, looking distinctly shaken by this news.

"But don't you see?" said Danny. "This is your chance, buddy boy! Obviously Madison dumped her ass the moment he found out she's pregnant. You could be her rebound, buddy!"

"You're crazy, Danny."

"No, I'm a genius. The two are often confused." He placed a hand on his colleague's shoulder. "This is your moment, Tommy. Your moment to shine!"

"Clearly she's still in love with the guy," said Tom miserably. "Just look at how red her eyes are. And how often she's been going to the bathroom. She's been crying her eyes out over Mad Madison. So why would she be interested in me?"

"She will be if you're the only decent person in this place. Madison is a jerk, and now is your chance to prove that you're a friend to her, not an idiot like him."

"I don't think so," said Tom, slumping lower and lower in his chair.

"Go over there now. Just talk to her. Show her a friendly face!"

But Tom sat there shaking his head, still stunned by this news.

So Danny finally rolled his eyes and continued his round.

"What does this mean, Max?" asked Dooley.

"This means we were right, Dooley. Tom is in love with Natalie, and if we can manage to bring these two together, Gabi will have solved two cases in one go."

"Gabi? Who's Gabi?"

"Dear Gabi. The *Gazette's* advice columnist? The reason why we're here in the first place?" And since he seemed to have a hard time understanding the intricacies of our assignment, I explained the whole thing to him once more. I must have been talking too loud, though, for when I looked up, I saw that half the office was looking in our direction, amused smiles on their collective faces.

Natalie even directed a watery smile at Tom, which he returned with some extra wattage added for good measure.

Now wouldn't that be something? That their shared interest in two caterwauling interning cats would bring these sundered hearts together?

CHAPTER 10

Vesta was trying to extract a decent cup of hot chocolate from the coffee machine in the office canteen when Natalie Ferrara walked in. The girl still looked pretty shook up, which wasn't surprising considering the trouble she was in.

"I can't seem to work this thing," Vesta grumbled as she punched a few buttons to no avail.

"Let me help you," said Natalie, and applied her gentle touch to the machine. "You need to be an old hand at this," she explained with a smile.

"I think you probably need a college degree to get it to spit out what you want." She eyed Natalie from the corner of her eye. "Are you all right, sweetie? You look a little under the weather, if you don't mind me saying so."

Natalie swallowed, then shook her head. "It's my brother. He lost his job and got kicked out of his apartment, so he's been staying with me. And he's a good kid, you know, but I live in a small flat, and it's not been easy sharing the space."

"I hear you," said Vesta. "I've been sharing a place with my daughter and her husband, and it's been an adjustment for all of us. I used to live alone, and giving up my own space was tough at first. Lucky for me they're both great people."

"You're the new senior intern, aren't you?"

"Vesta Muffin. And you're… Natalie? Madison's PA?"

Natalie nodded, offering Vesta a weak smile. "So how are you getting on? Settling in all right?"

"Oh, sure," Vesta assured the young woman. "I've been working for my son-in-law for years, you know, as his receptionist. Tex is a doctor, and I've been handling his roster of patients. So I never really retired."

Natalie frowned. "Tex Poole?"

"That's the one."

"A friend of mine is one of his patients."

"Best doctor in town, let me tell you. If you're ever in any trouble, he's the person to see."

Natalie nodded, and much to Vesta's surprise, tears had appeared in the girl's eyes. She quickly turned her face away, and wiped at her eyes. "I'm sorry," she said. "It's this whole business with my brother, you see. It's been pretty rough."

"Yeah, I can imagine," said Vesta. Though the business with the boss's baby was probably having an even worse effect on the young PA. She placed a hand on the woman's shoulder. "If you want to talk about it, I'm a good listener," she assured her.

Natalie nodded, but didn't speak. The machine had finished sputtering and spitting and had managed to produce something that looked like a hot cup of chocolate. Vesta took it and tried a sip. "This is some pretty good stuff," she said.

Natalie smiled. "You sound surprised. You shouldn't. Madison takes good care of his staff." Her smile faltered. "At least he tries to." And then she murmured an apology and quickly left the canteen, without even having taken a cup of coffee.

"Poor girl," said Vesta, shaking her head.

Scarlett was taking her mission seriously. She had grabbed a sheaf of documents from her desk and headed over to Tom Mitchell's desk. The kid looked up when she approached, and plastered a polite smile on his face.

"Hi, there," she said as she came walking up. "I'm hoping you could help me out with this. Someone from accounting gave me this printout, and I'm having trouble understanding what it is exactly that they want me to do."

"Well, let me see," said Tom as he took the stack of paper from her and placed them on his desk. He frowned as he studied the columns and columns of names and numbers. "So these are…"

"The names and addresses of subscribers who canceled their subscriptions," Scarlett supplied as she glanced in the direction of Natalie, who had just returned to her desk. From where Tom was sitting he had a perfect view of the PA, and also of Michael Madison, whose office was just beyond Natalie's desk.

"So what is it that accounting wants you to do with these?" asked Tom.

"They want me to cross-check this printout against this printout," said Scarlett, and dumped another stack of paper on Tom's desk. "These are the people who took advantage of the digital subscription offer, which is cheaper than the paper one."

"Okay, so what you want to do is—"

"Is that *Glimmer*?" asked Scarlett, pointing to the young man's computer.

"Yeah, I'm working on an article about spring cleaning," said Tom. "Why, do you read *Glimmer*?"

"Do I read *Glimmer*! I only devour the magazine, and have done since just about forever. In fact my mom subscribed to

Glimmer, and before her my grandma. You could say the Canyons made *Glimmer* what it is today."

"Loyal reader, huh?" said Tom. "I wish there were more of you."

"Readership is dropping?"

"Yeah, circulation numbers are down across the board." He smiled. "Which is why it's important to keep loyal readers like yourself happy and renewing their subscriptions. I'm Tom, by the way. And you're one of the new senior interns, correct?"

"Oh, how silly of me. Totally forgot to introduce myself! Yeah, my name is Scarlett, and me and my friend Vesta are Advantage's newest hires. Yay!"

"Welcome aboard, Scarlett. Glad to see a new face around here."

"Yeah, it means things can't be so bad, if Advantage is still hiring."

"Correct me if I'm wrong, but you are an intern, right? So not paid?"

"Yeah, Madison got a good deal when he got us. Lots of experience, and free of charge!"

At the mention of the name Madison, a cloud passed across Tom's visage, but it soon passed. "I think you'll fit right in. We're a great little bunch here at Advantage."

Scarlett noticed a post-it on Tom's desk. On it he had scribbled '15 Ways to Spice up Your Love Life.' "If you need any help with that, just holler," she said. "I can think of way more than fifteen ways to spice up your love life."

A blush spread across Tom's face. "You can?"

"Oh, absolutely. In fact I could show you ways no one has ever tried before except me." She leaned in. "I have an adventurous streak when it comes to enjoying the pleasures of the flesh."

Tom gulped a little. "Do you now?"

"There's things a man can do to a woman that will guarantee she will hang on to him forever, Tom." She spoke earnestly, looking deeply into the man's eyes. She had taken a seat at the edge of his desk, and was thinking that if only he'd get rid of those glasses he'd improve his attractiveness with at least a factor of ten.

"Things… a man can do to a woman?" he asked, adjusting his glasses.

"If you want, I could show you," she suggested, shifting her position on the desk. She'd popped a button or two on her blouse, and as she leaned in, there was a certain wiggling going on, and a certain jiggling, causing Tom to redden even more as he was granted a certain measure of insight into certain assets.

He cleared his throat. "I could use a few p-p-pointers, f-f-for sure."

"Well, that's settled, then," she said, leaning back again. She could see that the kid was suffering from an acute case of vertigo, and didn't want him to pass out on the office floor. "Why don't we get together this afternoon, and I'll share some of these insights with you, mh?"

"A-a-absolutely," he stuttered. "Too kind."

"No problem. See you later, Tommy."

"See you later… Scarlett."

CHAPTER 11

Dooley and I had returned to Natalie's desk, and decided to stick around for a while, picking up any clues we might gather as to the young woman's state of mind. I could see that Scarlett was 'working' on Tom, using her not inconsiderable charm to educate the young man on the ways of how to seduce a member of the opposite sex. But if Gran's plan was to be successful, we also had to disentangle Natalie's complicated love life, which probably was a lot harder to accomplish.

And as we settled in for the duration, a woman came stalking through the office with purposeful step, darted one scathing look at Natalie, then waltzed into Madison's office and slammed the door. Moments later the blinds were dropped, and Madison and his visitor were obscured from view.

"Oh, God," Natalie groaned. She clearly had recognized this visitor.

Gran, who didn't miss a trick, came hurrying up. "What's happening?" she asked.

"Madison's wife just arrived," said Natalie.

"Bad news?"

"Very."

Which is when the screaming began. We couldn't understand what was being said, but whatever it was, it wasn't happy or kind!

"Madison's marriage is in trouble, is it?" asked Gran.

"Oh, absolutely. Wouldn't surprise me if Deith is planning to divorce him."

"They've got kids? Madison and his wife?"

Natalie hesitated for a moment, then shook her head. "No kids."

"At least there's that. The moment kids are in the picture, it's that much harder."

Natalie darted a quick look to Gran, clearly wondering what she knew, but said nothing.

"He's something of a player, though, isn't he, Madison?" Gran continued to pry. "I mean, I don't know the guy, of course, but he looks like a real playboy."

"He's very loyal... to the woman he loves," said Natalie.

"Which isn't Deith?"

But Natalie wasn't to be drawn out so easily. "I wouldn't know about that," she insisted.

"Oh, come on. You've been the guy's PA for how long now?"

"Five years," said Natalie, fiddling with a ring on her finger.

"So you must know the guy inside and out."

"I take care of his professional life, not his personal one."

Gran nodded. "Of course you do, sweetie. Of course you do." She gave Natalie's arm a gentle squeeze, causing Natalie to cast down her eyes and bite down on her bottom lip. Her emotions were clearly very near to the surface, and she was afraid they would come spilling out under Gran's gentle nudging.

The door to Madison's office opened again, and his wife came stomping out, slammed the door behind her, and stalked off through the office once more, drawing all eyes to her, and causing people to start whispering furiously the moment she had passed.

"Looks like that divorce is happening sooner rather than later," Gran said.

Hope momentarily flashed across Natalie's face, and when Madison called her into his office, there was a pep in the young woman's step, causing Gran to comment, "Poor thing. She's still hung up on the guy, even though he's treating her like crap."

"If Madison gets a divorce, maybe he'll marry Natalie?" Dooley suggested.

"Never," said Gran. "Guys like Madison don't marry their secretaries."

"I thought Natalie was his personal assistant," I said.

"Different name, same job," said Gran, shaking her head.

She returned to her own desk, and so did we. And as we settled in, Scarlett came tripping over, a triumphant smile on her face. "I'm going to teach Tommy how to seduce a woman," she announced. "Natalie won't know what hit her!"

"Trust me when I tell you it's not that easy," said Gran. "That girl is still hung up on her boss. So much so he's got her pining for him, and hoping against hope that he'll take her back and make an honest woman out of her."

"Yeah, but he won't, right? And once she sees that, she'll snap out of it."

"It's going to take more than a few seduction techniques to make that girl fall out of love with Madison. She's head over heels, that one."

"Yeah, so is Tommy," said Scarlett. "Smitten like a kitten."

Dooley eyed me curiously. "I didn't know kittens could be smitten," he said.

"Only in the springtime," I said, causing Dooley to frown. Look, I know my answer wasn't satisfactory, but I had Natalie and Tom's happiness on my mind. No matter how experienced I might be as a detective, this matchmaking business was a whole other ball of wax! Navigating the complexities of human emotions and human relationships is a lot harder than cracking a murder case, let me tell you!

Just then, another person came stalking through the office. He was a tall man with thick dark hair and a noble sort of face. He was making a beeline for Madison's office, and didn't bother to knock or announce his arrival before entering.

We could see him planting his hands on Madison's desk, a departure from the norm of regular social behavior the big boss did not appreciate, judging from the furious look on the latter's face.

"So who's this bozo now?" asked Gran, a touch of frustration in her voice.

Lucky for us Danny the mailroom boy was on hand to enlighten us.

He must have heard Gran's outcry, for he materialized next to our desk and said, a glimmer of enjoyment in his eyes, "That, my dear ladies, is Gary Rapp."

"Who's he?" asked Gran bluntly.

"Gary is a fashion editor. Or rather was. Madison fired him last week. And my best guess is that he didn't take kindly to being summarily dismissed like that."

"So why did Madison can his ass?" asked Gran.

"Turns out Gary likes the ladies more than the ladies like him," said Danny, a little cryptically. When both Gran and Scarlett looked up at the kid with expectant looks on their faces, he elucidated, "For his job Gary spent a lot of time on photoshoots. Turns out he couldn't keep his hands to himself on many of these occasions. So when several models filed an official complaint with HR, Madison had no choice but to get rid of the guy. That kind of behavior might have been condoned once upon a time, but unfortunately for Mr. Rapp, times have changed."

"Good riddance," Gran grunted. She then turned to Danny, who clearly was the fount of information she had hoped he was. "Say, Danny. I heard a rumor that big boss Madison managed to get one of your colleagues pregnant. Any truth to that?"

Danny wiggled his eyebrows meaningfully. "Maybe it is, maybe it isn't."

"I'm guessing maybe it is. So who's the lucky lady?"

Danny directed a meaningful look at Natalie's back, and Scarlett and Gran gasped in shock. "No way," said Scarlett.

But Danny nodded. "Yes, way. Though now rumor has it that Gary might have had something to do with it."

"Gary Rapp is Natalie's baby daddy?" asked Gran.

"Shh! Not so loud!" Danny admonished her. "But yeah. It's the latest rumor that's been doing the rounds. Though my money is still on Madison."

"People are betting who the father is?" asked Scarlett.

"You didn't get this from me, but if you want in on the syndicate, just say the word. As of ten minutes ago, odds on Gary are five to one, Madison is ten to one."

"Looks like Madison's got the better odds, huh?" said Gran, nodding.

A loud noise had us all look up. Gary Rapp had slammed the door on his way out, with Natalie looking on with a fervent look on her face, cheeks flaming red.

Danny cursed under his breath. "Looks like Gary's stock has just gone up. Now I'll have to go and make the rounds again."

And indeed, several hands went up, beckoning the office

boy. People had evidently closely witnessed the scene, and were ready to change favorites!

"I think it's disgusting," said Scarlett. "Betting on a girl's happiness like that."

"Welcome to the world of office politics," said Gran. "Where fortunes are made or lost in the blink of an eye. Or the arrival or departure of a current favorite."

CHAPTER 12

Tex should have been in the office, but instead he was trolling through the neighborhood, collecting the letters a troop of girl scouts had delivered the day before. Marge had told him in no uncertain terms what she thought of a man who put his love letters to her in the trash, and this was his chance at redemption.

Harriet and Brutus were trailing him, and making sure he collected every last one of the letters. They were under strict instruction not to let Marge's husband out of their sight, since she didn't trust him any further right now than she could throw him. Whatever that meant.

Brutus thought it was a strange expression. Why would Marge want to throw Tex? He even thought it was probably physically impossible for a diminutive woman like Marge to throw a tall man like her husband. Unless she had suddenly developed superhuman strength, or had joined the ranks of the Marvel universe.

"Promise me you'll never write me any love letters, snuggle bear," Harriet now told her mate.

"I promise, sweet cheeks," said Brutus.

"I mean, imagine if our personal thoughts were distributed amongst all of our friends—or even worse, a bunch of complete strangers. It's too horrible to contemplate!"

"You do know that cats can't write, don't you, lemon drop?" asked Brutus with a touch of concern. "We don't have the opposable thumbs to hold a pen."

"I know that, love sponge. But still. Just for my own peace of mind, promise me you'll never, ever put your personal musings about our relationship on paper."

"I promise," said Brutus fervently, and he meant it, too.

"Thank you, Mrs. Jackson," said Tex as he accepted the letter from the older lady.

"You have very nice handwriting, Doctor Poole," said Mrs. Jackson. "I could understand nearly everything you wrote. There's just one passage that wasn't clear to me. What did you mean by 'I want to be your Tampax?'"

Tex swallowed once or twice. "I'm sure you must have misread, Mrs. Jackson."

"I don't think so. I distinctly remember reading it and wondering what it meant. I even asked my friend Mrs. Jones, and she said it probably referred to a tampon. And I said you couldn't possibly be referring to a tampon, since the rest of your letter was very sweet, but also very sexy, if you know what I mean. And tampons may be a lot of things, but they're not sexy or sweet, are they now?"

"No," said Tex. "No, I guess not."

He was sweating profusely, Brutus saw, and he felt for the guy.

"This is probably the most humiliating thing I've ever seen," he told his girlfriend. "Poor Tex. I feel for him."

"I'd feel more for him if he hadn't put those letters out for trash collection," said Harriet, and Brutus could see his girlfriend was as implacable as Marge had been. And suddenly he felt relieved that cats couldn't write. Imagine having the whole world made privy to your personal thoughts about tampons and such. He shivered as Tex said his goodbyes to Mrs. Jackson, and slumped off.

"Only two more to go," the good doctor announced, trying to put on a brave face. But Brutus could see that his heart wasn't in it.

Clearly this was not the doctor's finest hour.

※

Odelia, who'd finished up an article on the best herbs and spices to make the perfect pumpkin soup, waltzed into her uncle's office down at the police precinct.

Uncle Alec looked up when his niece entered and looked relieved to see her. "What brings you here?" he asked as he leaned back in his chair and intertwined his hands behind his head.

"Boredom, to be honest," said Odelia, dropping down on a chair. "Dan's got me writing articles about pumpkin soup now."

"That bad, huh?"

"Nothing's happening in this town, Uncle Alec. Nothing at all!"

"I know," said her uncle, but instead of looking bored, he looked relieved. "What?" he added when he saw the look on his niece's face. "It's a good thing when the police have nothing to do. It means no crimes are being committed, and everyone is happy and going about their business without bothering anyone else."

"No neighbors threatening to kill each other? No wives threatening to shoot their husbands?"

"Nothing at all," said Uncle Alec. "And that's exactly the way it should be."

"If nothing is happening, I've got nothing to write about," Odelia grumbled. "And if I've got nothing to write about, we don't have a paper."

"I'm sorry, honey. But you can't expect me to make up some imaginary crime, just so you and Dan can fill your paper, do you now?"

"No, I guess not," she said reluctantly. She idly swiveled in her swivel chair. "Guess I'll have to write a couple more articles about how to make the perfect pumpkin soup."

"What's your gran been up to? Chase told me she's interning at *Glimmer*?"

"Yeah, she and Scarlett are trying to heal a broken heart, apparently. Max and Dooley are on the case, so I'm going to hear all about it tonight." She grimaced. "Fat lot of good it'll do me. I can't write an article about a secretary who's pregnant with her boss's baby, or some guy who's in love with his colleague."

"No, I guess not," said Uncle Alec. Then he brightened. "Marge told me about that letter business. Now there's the perfect story for the *Gazette*. It's got romance, it's got human interest, some excitement, the whole shebang."

"It also has my mom and dad involved. Mom already warned me not to write an article about those letters, or else she'll never invite me over for dinner again."

"Yeah, I guess it is all very personal—not to mention very painful for everyone involved." He couldn't suppress a grin, though, and soon they were both laughing, as they imagined Tex going door to door to try and get his precious letters back!

"If this had happened to anyone else, Dan would have me writing all about it," she said. "But seeing as it hits too close to home..."

Just then, her uncle's phone chimed, and he gave it a

furtive look, then glanced through the window in the direction of Town Hall, located across Town Square.

"Message from Charlene?" asked Odelia.

Her uncle nodded. "She's got a new… project she wants to discuss with me." He got up with some effort and put his phone in his pocket.

"What project? Something important?"

"Nah, nothing special. You know, just some project. The usual stuff."

She had a feeling her uncle wasn't being entirely honest with her, but decided to let it go. Everyone has a right to a private life, much though she would have loved to pry into this love affair between the town's mayor and chief of police.

Gah. Now that was exactly the trouble when you knew everyone in town: you started to be hampered in your ambitions as an investigative reporter!

※

Alec slipped into the Mayor's office and quietly closed the door behind him. On the desk, the Mayor herself was seated, dressed in a long overcoat. A mysterious smile was playing about her lips. He knew that smile. It meant she was up to something!

"You wanted to see me, Madam Mayor?" he asked politely.

"Yes, Chief Lip," said the Mayor. "There's an urgent matter we need to discuss."

"Is that a fact, Madam Mayor?"

"A matter of life and death, in fact."

"Oh, my. That sounds important, Madam Mayor."

"Come here, Chief Lip," the Mayor summoned. "And be seated."

The Chief approached the desk, licking his lips as he did. "Yes, Madam Mayor."

"Did you read the article?"

"I did, Madam Mayor."

"Then you know the drill. Get down, Chief!"

The Chief got down.

"On the floor! On your hands and knees!"

The Chief proceeded as instructed.

"What are you going to do with me, pray tell?" he asked, looking up at the figure towering over him.

In one swift motion, Charlene threw off the overcoat. Underneath, she was dressed in a black leather outfit. It was a shiny thing she had found on some internet site specializing in BDSM outfits. And as he marveled at how well the getup suited her, she extracted a whip from the recesses of her costume, and slashed the air with it. It made a delicious cracking sound.

"Now kneel, you scum!" the Mayor bellowed, cracking the whip once more.

And so kneel he did.

Just then, the door opened and Charlene's secretary Imelda entered. When the older woman caught sight of the two of them, Charlene in her leather outfit, and Uncle Alec on the floor, that whip held high above the Mayor's head, she goggled for a moment, then quickly stepped back again, murmured an apology, and closed the door.

Charlene sighed. "Oh, Alec. I thought you locked the door?"

"I did," said Alec.

"Looks like I'll have to get it fixed again."

He grinned up at her, and she returned the grin, then cracked the whip again. "You're going to get punished for this, you know that, right?"

"Can't wait, my love," said Alec softly.

CHAPTER 13

Marge was bored. Afternoons were usually her busiest time, with plenty of her regulars coming in and checking out their favorite books. Now, though, she hadn't seen anyone for the past hour. Not even Mrs. Samson, who came in every day. Maybe reading that letter Tex wrote yesterday had spooked the old lady.

Thinking about that letter had Marge silently fuming again. Tex had apologized, but only after she had made it clear how humiliating the experience was, or how hurtful that he would simply throw out the letters that had established their relationship in the first place. How unthinkingly unkind.

Tex had assured her he hadn't wanted to throw out those letters. That they must have accidentally ended up on the sidewalk. Or maybe Chase had put them out, thinking it was just some old junk. Still, it was perhaps a sign? A sign that their relationship had seen better days and wasn't what it used to be?

And as she turned the events round and round in her mind, who would suddenly walk in but Gary Rapp! The same guy who'd been in yesterday, making such flattering and complimentary comments. Now here was a man who knew how to make a woman feel good about herself. A man, in other words, who was the exact opposite of Marge's husband, who simply took her for granted, and even went so far as to throw the foundation stone of their marriage into the garbage.

"Well, hello," said Gary as he approached the desk. He was carrying the books she'd given him yesterday.

"You finished those already?" she asked.

"I'm a fast reader," he said with a warm smile. "And I have to say, you weren't kidding when you told me I'd love these. I did, and now of course I was wondering if you can give me some more good advice."

"Absolutely," she said. "I can show you a few more that I'm sure you will like."

And as she took him to the romance department, she became aware of his presence behind her, and knew he was checking her out. It supplied her with a frisson of excitement. It had been so long that a man had looked at her like that, she'd completely forgotten what it felt like. And she had to admit it felt good!

She showed Gary a few books she thought he would like, and he took them all. Then he turned to her. "Could I perhaps entice you to have dinner with me?" When she opened her mouth to protest, he quickly held up his hand. "Just to talk some more about books, I promise you. I know you're married, and coming between you and your husband is the furthest thing from my mind."

"I can't, Gary. I'm sorry."

"I understand," he said, graciously accepting her refusal. "If you change your mind..."

"I won't," she assured him.

"Clearly you have a husband who makes you happy," he

said. She wavered, and he continued, "Which is exactly what you deserve, Marge. A woman like you deserves a husband who treats her like a queen. Makes sure she's feeling loved and taken care of every moment of every day." He took her hand. The warmth of his touch seeped into her hand, and instead of pulling back, she thought it felt good to be touched like that. With reverence. With respect. "Just promise me you'll think about it," he said.

She found herself nodding. "Thanks, Gary. You're very sweet."

"Not sweet," he corrected her. "I think smitten is a better word."

And like a kid of fifteen, she actually blushed!

Oh, how silly she was being!

He leaned in, then, but before their lips touched, she broke the spell by turning her head away. "I couldn't," she said quietly, and so instead he kissed her hand.

What a perfect gentleman, she thought once he'd left. She felt all fluttery, and her legs had turned to jelly.

Just then, her phone chimed, and she picked up. "Yes, Tex?"

"I got your letters back," he announced, sounding a little breathless. "Every last one of them."

"Well, that's good," she said absentmindedly, looking at the hand where Gary had placed that kiss. She could still feel the touch of his lips.

"And I promise you this will never happen again, Marge."

"It better not," she said.

"Though I think Mrs. Jackson made a copy of one of the letters. The one about the tampon? She seemed really intrigued by it. Couldn't stop asking questions."

In spite of herself, she had to smile. "Oh, Tex," she sighed.

Harriet listened to Tex explaining to Marge about their letter retrieval expedition. She was thoroughly bored with the entire incident by now. How silly humans were. And how petty. Just because a couple of letters had escaped into the wild they had to go and make a big fuss about it. Who cared about some old letters from thirty years ago? And besides, it wasn't Tex's fault, was it? In fact it could have happened to anyone.

"Humans," she told her boyfriend. "They just love to make a mountain out of a molehill every single time, don't they? Drama, drama, drama."

They were back at the house, with Tex pacing the living room, and Harriet and Brutus on the couch. Which is when Harriet caught Brutus staring at her for some reason. Her heart stopped. "What is it? Is something wrong with me, precious?"

"There's something on your nose," said Brutus.

Her heart stopped—or at least that's how it felt.

"What is it?! Tell me!" she demanded.

"A spot," said Brutus. "Just a tiny spot, really."

She uttered a wail of despair, then flew off the couch, and up the stairs. In the bathroom, she jumped the sink in one swift movement and moments later was staring at her reflection in the mirror. And that's when she saw it. A big red spot had appeared on the bridge of her nose.

"Nooooooooooo!" she cried in agony.

It wasn't a small spot, like Brutus said. It was a big spot. In fact the spot was all she could see, as it seemed to cover her entire face!

It was red, it was angry, and it looked as if someone had slashed her face with a sharp razor.

And with her photoshoot only days away, it was the worst

possible moment for this horrible blemish to appear on her lovely visage.

Brutus, who'd silently snuck into the bathroom, glanced up at her. "It's not so bad, is it?" he asked—the traitor!

"It is bad!" she wailed. "It's horrible. It's a tragedy—the worst thing to happen to me ever!"

"It'll pass," he said. "Just you wait and see. This time tomorrow it'll be gone."

"No, it won't. It'll keep on growing and growing and growing—like a pumpkin. And just when I've got to be ready for my shoot, I'll look like a monster! A terrible, hideous monster!"

"No, you won't. And besides, these photographers have all kinds of tricks to deal with these contingencies. I'll bet he's got a cream or whatever to cover that spot right up. And then of course there's Photoshop."

She was only partly reassured by his words. "It's the end of the world," she told him in a quiet voice as she prostrated herself across the sink. "The end of my life!"

CHAPTER 14

Interesting things had been happening at Advantage Publishing all day long, and the number of people in and out of Madison's office was growing by the minute. The man certainly led an interesting life!

And all throughout the events that unfolded, Danny kept us informed.

Shortly before lunch, a man named Wayne Piscina had been fired. According to Danny some old homophobic and racist tweets had surfaced, which led to a big furor online, and Wayne, who worked as an assistant photographer, had to go.

Next, a rumor circulated that Advantage Publishing and Madison himself were being sued by a model. The model's name was Ona Konpacka, and according to Danny the woman's face was permanently disfigured because of a botched cosmetic procedure. Danny showed us pictures of the woman, and it has to be said she was gorgeous. Now, apparently, not so much—though there were no pictures to indicate the damage that was done. No before and after.

"Apparently she had a bad reaction to some fillers that were injected into her face," Danny explained to an eager audience of four. "The fillers permanently altered the shape, and now she won't leave the house. Her career is ruined, her life is over, and she's suing Advantage Publishing and Madison for millions."

"But why? It's not Madison's fault that the surgeon botched the procedure," said Scarlett, who kept touching her face as Danny related this horror story.

"Oh, but she's suing the surgeon, too, of course, and the clinic. But she says Madison personally told her to get the procedure, since he wasn't happy about the way she looked, and said she could stay relevant only if she had some minor alterations. And also, he was the one who recommended this particular clinic."

"Poor woman," said Scarlett as she studied Miss Konpacka's face. "Imagine having your face destroyed by some horrible butcher. She'll never work again?"

"As far as I understood, the structure of her face is so different now even her own mother doesn't recognize her anymore," said Danny. He seemed to relish relating the details of this latest example of a cosmetic procedure gone wrong.

"A boyfriend once told me to get fillers, and I declined," said Scarlett, gently fingering her lips. "Thank God I did. Though I had some minor work done, I never did fillers."

"And you better not," said Gran. "Look what happened to this model." She glanced over to Madison, who was pacing his office, screaming something into his phone, which was one of those wireless models, with something stuck in his ear.

Up and down his office he went, and even though we couldn't understand what he was saying, it was obvious the man was under tremendous pressure.

Natalie was also studying her boss, and I thought I could detect from her body language that she felt for her former lover and baby daddy. Now that he was in trouble, she was clearly eager to kiss his head and make the trouble go away.

And behind Natalie, Tom was staring at the PA, and it was pretty obvious what he was thinking: that he wanted to be the one to shower the girl with kisses and make all her trouble go away. But from the young man's demeanor, it was also clear he didn't think that would ever happen.

Danny had left, to spread some more gossip around the office, and take bets, and Scarlett and Gran, even though they should have been correcting spreadsheets, were conferring about the next step in their rescue operation.

"This place is better than any soap I've ever seen," said Scarlett. "Better than *The Bold and the Beautiful* or *General Hospital*. We should have gone back to work a long time ago. This is so much fun!"

"If you remember, I never stopped working," Gran pointed out.

"Being Tex's receptionist doesn't count," said Scarlett.

"It does, too. It's hard work having to listen to Tex's patients all day."

"I worked for Tex, and I don't remember it as work. Tex is a sweetheart, and the kindest, best employer ever."

"Yeah, that's true," Gran admitted. "Tex is a sweetheart. Not like Madison, who seems like some kind of ogre."

They eyed the big boss for a moment, then returned to the topic at hand.

"So what do you reckon Tom's chances are?" asked Gran.

"Zero," said Scarlett. "The kid's nice, but he's got as much charm as a dish towel."

"Yeah, and judging from the way Natalie keeps looking at Madison, I don't think she's ready to move on." She sighed deeply. "Looks like this mission of Dear Gabi on the Road is going to be a bust, honey."

"Oh, well. Better luck next time, I guess."

※

Vesta had wandered into the canteen for a refill. She couldn't get over the fact that she could drink as much hot chocolate as she liked, and didn't have to pay for it. Working for the man had its perks, and if she ever went back to working for Tex, the first thing she'd do was ask him to install a decent hot chocolate maker.

Danny was seated at the table when she walked in, and greeted her with a big grin. "Tommy tells me your friend has been trying to teach him how to seduce the ladies?"

"Yeah, Scarlett is good at that kind of stuff," Vesta admitted. "Though she seems to feel it's going to be a bust."

"I'm afraid she's probably right. I've been trying to get Tommy to ask Natalie out for months, and he's been stalling me."

"You know Tommy well, do you?"

"He's my cousin," said Danny, much to Vesta's surprise. "In fact we live together. Him and his mom and his little brother."

"You all live together?"

"Yeah, it's a long story. My mom and dad died when I was little, and Auntie Mel has been my second mom ever since. So Tom and Harry, that's Tom's little brother, are like brothers to me. We all grew up together under the same roof."

"So you know about his affections for Natalie, huh?"

The mailroom clerk rolled his eyes. "Do I? It's all he ever talks about!"

"Looks like Natalie's got a thing for the big boss, though."

"Yeah, it's been like that from the day she started here. But Madison is married, and he's not about to get a divorce so he can make an honest woman out of sweet little Natalie." He grimaced. "Which is eating Tommy alive, as you can imagine."

"He does look very unhappy with the whole situation. How did he react when he found out Natalie is pregnant?"

"I just told him this morning. He did not take it well. Especially when I told him Madison is probably the father. He didn't seem to believe me."

Vesta, who didn't like to admit defeat, frowned into her cup. "Okay, so what if you and me and Scarlett—we all make one final effort to get Tom to ask Natalie out. Do you think he'll do it?"

Danny shrugged. "Honestly? I don't know."

"Let's just give it another shot," Vesta suggested. "And if it doesn't work, we'll drop it."

"Deal," said Danny, and held up his fist for a fist bump, which Vesta awkwardly obliged. Young people these days. What was wrong with a simple handshake?

❧

When Gran returned from the canteen, her eyes were shining, and she looked like a woman with a plan. Danny was trailing in her wake, and I just knew what was about to happen.

"Uh-oh," I said.

"What's going on?" asked Dooley, who had been napping next to me.

"I think they're going to try to make Tom ask Natalie out on a date."

"Oh, so that's good, isn't it?"

"I'm not sure." I glanced in Natalie's direction. The young PA sat ramrod straight at her desk, and was typing on her computer at a relentless pace, her fingers dancing across the keyboard. There were red spots on her cheekbones, and I had the impression she was a woman on the verge of a nervous breakdown.

But Gran and Scarlett and Danny didn't see it that way. And so we watched the small contingent move over to Tom's desk. The kid listened, shook his head a few times, looked at Natalie's back a couple of times more, and finally stood, urged on by the trio. He seemed to gather his courage, and made his way over to Natalie.

For a few moments, he stood chatting to her, then must have popped the question, for Natalie jerked her head around, to give him a look of utter astonishment. Moments later she shook her head, Tom slumped in response, and as he returned to his desk, we could see she'd taken the wind right out of his sails.

"I guess that's a hard no," said Dooley.

"Yeah, looks like," I agreed.

Tom dropped down in his chair like a bag of potatoes, and all the claps on the back and words of advice couldn't cheer him up. In fact he looked worse now than he had all day. At least before he was holding onto some measure of hope to buoy him. Now there was no more hope. The girl of his dreams had turned him down flat. And that, as they say, was that!

"Oh, well, at least he tried," I said, as I put my head on my paws again.

"Yeah, at least there's that," Dooley said. "Did you know that a magazine like *Glimmer* has a circulation of one million copies, Max? That's one million people reading the magazine every single month. That's a lot of people, isn't it? Though not as much as *Good Housekeeping*, which has a circulation of four million! Four million people reading the magazine every single month. Can you imagine?"

I could, and somehow hearing all these numbers made me tired. And so while Dooley kept droning off names and numbers, I soon drifted off to sleep.

Odd, that. How a busy office can induce such a wonderful nap. Makes you wonder how sleeplessness can exist, in a world filled with offices like that.

CHAPTER 15

After a long day of hard labor at the office, one expects to arrive home to a delicious meal, before settling in to watch one's favorite show, and taking a well-deserved nap on the couch, surrounded by one's loved ones.

Instead we arrived in what amounted to an atmosphere of sheer pandemonium!

Harriet was experiencing a major crisis, and the moment we got back from Advantage Publishing, we were all bundled into Gran's car and taken, at a high rate of speed, to Vena Aleman, our local veterinarian.

"I'm dead!" Harriet lamented. "This is the end, I'm dead!"

"It's just a spot," Brutus was saying. "Just a minor, little spot."

"It's cancer—I just know it is. It's cancer and it's spreading!"

"It's not cancer, Harriet," said Gran, who was trying her darndest to keep her eyes on the road, while at the same time having to keep Harriet's panic attack at bay.

"It's cancer of the nose," Harriet insisted. "And it's spreading everywhere!" She directed a pleading look at her mate. "Brutus, I'm so grateful to have known you. The only regret I have is that we didn't meet sooner. That we had so precious little time."

"It's not cancer," Brutus insisted stubbornly, but I could see he was starting to waver. "Is it, Max?"

"I'm not a doctor," I said, as I studied the spot more closely. "It could be cancer, or it could not. Hard to know for sure."

"If a spot has a weird shape and a weird color it's almost certainly cancer," Dooley announced. "And this spot looks very weird to me, and it has a very weird color, too." He placed a consoling paw on Harriet's arm. "It's been wonderful knowing you, Harriet. Rest assured we'll always remember you with fondness."

"Oh, God!" Harriet wailed. "I'm dying—this is the end for me! And just when I looked my absolute best!"

"You do look your absolute best," Brutus said, nervously looking at Gran, hoping for some measure of reassurance from the old lady. None was forthcoming, though, for Gran had shifted into higher gear, and the car was hurtling along the road at breakneck speed, almost clipping a few pedestrians and even a couple of cyclists in the process.

"Just when my big break finally came," Harriet lamented as she placed a paw to her brow and closed her eyes, "fate caught up with me. I was destined for greatness, but it simply was not to be. Promise me white roses, sweetness."

"Plenty of white roses," Brutus promised.

"And a funeral fit for royalty."

"Absolutely," Brutus said.

"Is she really dying, Max?" asked Dooley as Brutus took his mate's paw and patted it consolingly.

"I doubt it, Dooley," I said. "Harriet is one of those cats who will never die. She's a diva, you see. And we all know that divas outlive us all, in spite of all the drama." Or perhaps because of it. Ordinary folk like you and me keep all that drama inside, while the Harriets of this world let it spill out at every available opportunity, transferring the bulk of their tragedy onto the shoulders of others.

We finally arrived at Vena's, and lucky for us, there was no one in the waiting room, so we were ushered straight into the doctor's main office, where she patiently awaited us, a sardonic smile on her face. You can say about Vena what you will—and I know that in the past I've called her a vicious butcher, a cruel sadist and a cat's worst nightmare—but the woman always keeps her cool.

"So what do we have here?" she asked now as Gran hoisted Harriet onto the operating table and Vena moved in to take a closer look at that suspicious spot.

"It's cancer, isn't it?" asked Harriet nervously. "How long do I have? Weeks? Days? HOURS?!"

And then the most amazing thing happened. Vena frowned as she studied the spot, then performed a sort of flicking motion with her index finger, and said, "There. All gone."

We exchanged puzzled and confused glances.

"All gone? What do you mean, all gone?" Gran demanded.

"Just a bit of dried food," Vena explained. She gave Harriet an admonishing wag of her finger. "Looks like someone hasn't been grooming herself as thoroughly as she could have, mh?" She then directed a critical look at Gran. "And looks like some pet parent hasn't been conscious of their basic duty of care."

For once in her life Gran actually managed to look sheepish and apologetic. "I had a busy day," she said. "So when Harriet told me she had a suspicious spot, I didn't look any further but bundled her into the car and drove straight here."

"Harriet 'told' you this, did she?" said Vena with a slight smile.

"Well, I mean she didn't actually 'tell' me, of course," said Gran, grinning nervously. "But... well, you know what I mean."

"I do know what you mean," said Vena with a wink at the old lady. "And now that you're here, I think it's best if I take a closer look at the entire clowder."

And so, all because Harriet hadn't bothered to lick her nose after her most recent meal, we were all subjected to Vena's obnoxious prods and pokes!

Life isn't fair sometimes. It really is not!

CHAPTER 16

To say that Tex had lived through better days would be an understatement. Even though he'd managed to collect every last one of his letters, and had even offered them to Marge with the original ribbon wrapped around them in a nice bow, Marge had refused the present with untypical coolness.

And so it was that the good doctor sat in the kitchen, drowning his sorrow with a glass of apple juice, when Vesta walked in and found him like that.

Since she'd had to corral four cats through a thorough medical examination—never their favorite pastime—and had had to accept defeat at work that day, suffice it to say she wasn't feeling like some Florence Nightingale of old. Still, the moment she caught sight of her son-in-law's sad face, her mother's heart bled.

"Don't tell me you've got cancer, too," were her first words as she started making herself a cup of hot chamomile tea—a habit before retiring for the night.

Tex looked up. "Cancer? Who's got cancer?"

"Harriet thought she had skin cancer. Turns out it was a

piece of dried food stuck to her nose." She shook her head. "If all cancers were as easily removed as hers, our work at the doctor's office would be a lot easier."

"Marge refused to take back my letters," said Tex sadly. He gestured to the little pile on the kitchen table.

"So you got them all back, did you?" said Vesta, picking up the collection and idly rifling through it.

"I did. Took me all afternoon, but I finally managed." He sighed deeply. "I'll never be able to face these people again. Even Ted Trapper stopped me in the street to tell me how much he admired my penmanship. And if I'd considered publishing my letters. Said they'd be a big hit in certain circles."

"What circles? What is he talking about?"

"He says a lot of guys have trouble expressing their feelings to their prospective girlfriends, and my letters would be a great primer on the subject. His exact words were, 'There's gold in them thar hills, Poole!'"

Vesta grinned as she poured hot water from the kettle into her favorite 'Greatest Grandma in the World' cup. It was the same cup Odelia had gifted her many years ago, when she was just a little girl. Vesta took great care of that cup, and didn't let anyone else touch it. "Maybe he's right," she said. "Maybe there is gold in them thar hills. Good old-fashioned love letters may have gone out of fashion in this day and age of tweets and texts and WhatsApp, but I still think there's nothing more romantic for a girl than receiving a long letter from a boy."

"I guess," said Tex, but clearly his head wasn't in monetizing his letters, but in reconciling the girl he'd written them for in the first place—many years ago.

"Look, if you want to show how sorry you are, and get Marge to forgive you," said Vesta, as she took a seat at the kitchen table, "you need to do something more than simply return those letters to her. You need to wow her, buddy. Show her how much you still care—you do still care about my daughter, don't you?"

"Of course I do! Even after twenty-five years Marge is still the only one for me."

"I believe you," said Vesta. "But it's not enough to say it. You have to show it. Make her feel your affection. And the best way to do that is by—"

"Buying her dinner? Giving her a foot rub?"

"—saying it with—"

"Diamonds? Lingerie?"

"—flowers!"

Tex stared at her. "Flowers?" he asked, as if the concept was alien to him.

"Buy Marge a nice bouquet of flowers. Or better yet, buy her several. You'll see how she'll perk right up."

"Is that so?" said Tex. If anyone had perked up, it was him. Clearly the notion of not having to splurge on diamonds or lingerie appealed to his tightwad nature.

"You do know what Marge's favorite flowers are, don't you?"

"Um…"

"Oh, Tex. How long have you known my daughter?"

He gave her a sheepish look. "Long enough to know what kind of flowers she likes?"

"Roses, Tex. Especially the pink variety. So if Marge were to arrive home from work tomorrow, and find her house festooned with roses in every shade of pink, I think she'd forgive you that silliness with those letters of yours in a heartbeat."

Which actually gave her an idea. If she could figure out what kind of flower Natalie Ferrara liked, and whisper the idea in Tom Mitchell's ear…

"Where do I buy so many flowers?" Tex mused.

"Oh, Tex. Do I have to do everything for you? Just buy them online."

"Online?" he said with a frown.

"Yes, online. You order them, and they deliver them." She drained the last of her cup and got up. "Just do it."

"But…"

"See you tomorrow, Tex. I'm beat. Who knew working all day was so exhausting?"

And so she left her son-in-law googling 'How to buy flowers online,' and turned in for the night. She was feeling invigorated. This flower business could just turn this whole situation around. All Tom had to do was buy Natalie her favorite flowers, and maybe—just maybe—Dear Gabi could still work a miracle!

CHAPTER 17

One house over, Odelia and Chase were reading in bed, though it was actually Odelia who was reading a novel, with Chase sitting and staring at her, which she could detect from the corner of her eye. When she finally looked up, and found him grinning at her like an idiot, she frowned. "Is everything all right, babe?"

"Never better," Chase assured her. "In fact I feel so great I could sing!"

"Please don't," she implored, remembering how he'd once serenaded her, at the instigation of her dad, and had been hit by a disapproving shoe from their neighbor Kurt Mayfield.

"I feel great," Chase repeated. "Life is just so grand, isn't it? Life is amazing!"

She placed a hand on her hubby's brow. He didn't seem to have a fever. "I think you're coming down with something," she said. "Maybe you should see my dad tomorrow."

"I saw your dad today."

"I know. The letter business."

He made a dismissive gesture with his hand. "That's all

taken care of. Your dad got his letters back, gave them to your mom, and all is forgiven and forgotten."

Judging from the version of affairs her mom had given her, all was far from forgiven and forgotten, but there seemed no sense in bringing all that up now. "You're sure you're all right? You were acting weird this morning, too."

"I like to think I'm finally acting like my true self," he said, that big grin still plastered all across his face. "I'm finally coming into my own. Being the real me!"

If this was the real Chase, she wondered what had happened to the old one. She wanted him back! "You haven't made a drug bust recently, have you?" And sampling some of those illegal substances?

"Nope. No drug bust. The streets of Hampton Cove are as clean and safe as they ever were. In fact no crimes are being committed in this town. We're probably the most crime-free town in America right now. And it's all thanks to a positive mental attitude." He punched the air with his fist. "Yes, we can, babe!"

And to show them that she wholeheartedly agreed, Grace chose that moment to open her mouth and start loudly wailing.

At the foot of the bed, two cats stirred and opened sleepy eyes.

"When is that child ever going to start behaving like a normal human being?" Max lamented, not for the first time.

"Yes, when is she ever going to turn into a normal person?" Dooley wanted to know.

Odelia swung her feet from the bed, but Chase beat her to it. In a flash, he was out of the bed and picking Grace up from her own little bed and cradling her in his arms. "There, there," he murmured softly. "Daddy's here, my sweet little princess."

There was something to be said for this new, improved Chase, Odelia thought as she watched him comfort their baby girl. It might be a little scary, as it was a far cry from the sometimes grumpy Chase Kingsley she'd come to know and love, but Grace seemed to respond well to Chase 2.0.

He gave her a dazzling smile. "All she needed was her daddy," he said, as Grace mumbled something and went back to sleep. And as he put her to bed, he said, "Your dad was right. Never let them see you sad. Some great advice right there."

She frowned. "Wait, what?"

"Your dad? I asked him for advice on being a dad, seeing as he was such a great dad to you? And he told me to become Mr. Positivity. Always exude cheerfulness and a positive mental attitude in front of the kid. And I have to say, it works like a charm." He grimaced and rubbed his cheek. "It's hard on the facial muscles, though, all this smiling. Guess I'm not used to it."

Now it was her turn to smile. "You asked Dad for his advice on being a dad?"

"I did. I mean, you turned out such a wonderful person, so he must have done something right, right?"

"I guess so," she said. "Though Mom might have had something to do with that, too, and Gran, of course."

At the mention of Gran, Chase grimaced. Clearly his opinion of Gran's parental skills wasn't as high as it could have been.

"And of course every child has its own personality. I had mine, and Grace has hers, which is going to be different from ours. Not sure there's a lot we can do about that—no matter how often we smile, or display a positive mental attitude."

His smile faltered, but then was back in full force. "Tex raised you to be a strong, independent, wonderful human being, and I'm determined to do the same with Grace. And if I have to grin like an idiot every time she's with me, then so be it."

Odelia pressed a loving arm to her husband's shoulder. "You don't have to grin like an idiot to be a good dad, Chase. You are a good person, and a great dad."

This time his smile vanished, and was replaced by a look of sheer anguish. "But what if I screw it up? I only have one shot at this, babe. And I don't want to ruin it. I don't want to look back on my life and realize I was a terrible dad."

"You couldn't be a terrible dad if you tried. And neither am I going to be a terrible mom. Are we going to make mistakes? Sure. But we're going to learn from them, and be the best parents we can be. Same way we're trying to be the best people we can be. Because that's who we are."

"Mh." He didn't look convinced. "If only my dad were still alive. He would have loved to be a grandad."

"I'm sure he's looking down on us from up there, knowing you're doing a good job and being proud of you, babe."

Chase let out a deep sigh, and folded his arms behind his head. "It's tough having to be positive all the time. And not just on my facial muscles."

"You just be you," she suggested. "And I'll be me, and we'll both figure it out as we go along. How is that for advice?"

"Very wise," he said, and planted a grateful kiss on her cheek. "Just like you."

"And besides, my dad wasn't exactly Mr. Positivity. If I remember correctly, he could be grumpy from time to time, especially when things didn't work out at the office, or when Gran was being, well, Gran. And somehow I still ended up being a normal person and not an ax murderer, right?"

"Right," he said with a grin. "I can definitely confirm you're not an ax murderer."

And on that positive note, she switched off her bedside light, and they turned in for the night.

CHAPTER 18

Once our humans had finally gone to sleep—which took them long enough, I have to say—and they had extinguished the light, it was time for Dooley and myself to head on out for that most important time: cat choir time!

We had a lot to talk about, with our adventures at the office, and Harriet's spot, which turned out not to be as life-threatening as she had thought, and I think we were all eager to relate our experience to our friends.

"Are you sure you should walk all the way to the park, Harriet?" asked Dooley. "Your paws are going to get dirty, and you have to keep them clean for your shoot."

Harriet gave Dooley a sideways glance, to ascertain if he wasn't pulling her tail. She should have known better. Dooley doesn't have a single ounce of cynicism in him, or sarcasm, and was genuinely concerned about Harriet's appearance.

"I can lick my paws clean, thank you very much," she said. "And besides, that shoot is still days away, so I can afford to get a little dirty. Gran told me the people that run the shoot have an entire team ready and waiting to spruce me right up."

"Oh, just like with movie stars, you mean?" asked Dooley.

"Exactly like with movie stars!" said Harriet, her excitement increasing with leaps and bounds now that she was talking about her favorite subject: herself. "They're going to primp me to within an inch of my life before they're through." She sighed happily. "I'm going to look the very best I've ever looked. And that's even before they apply all of that Photoshop stuff to the final results. This cover is going to be one for the books. One to save for posterity. Something to treasure."

It was nice to see her happy again, after the cancer scare she'd had, but I couldn't help but wonder if this shoot would actually happen. After having taken a peek at the inner workings of Advantage Publishing—a look behind the curtain, so to speak—they seemed to be a company facing a multitude of problems. Such as there were: a publicist quitting her job, a fashion editor being fired for harassing his models, a former supermodel suing the company and its CEO for ruining her face, and an assistant embroiled in a scandal over some old tweets.

And then there was the mysterious fight with Mrs. Madison, and the general image I got from Mr. Madison was that of a man under extreme duress.

Would Advantage Publishing still exist by the time Harriet's shoot was supposed to happen? Was the captain of the ship capable of righting his boat? Or was Advantage going under, mired in scandal? Or was this just par for the course? Just another day at the office?

One wondered how Michael Madison slept at night, with so much going on.

"So how was your day?" asked Brutus finally, when Harriet had finished extolling the virtues of herself.

"Oh, so so," I said.

"Gran is trying to match a shy editor with a sad secretary," Dooley explained. "The sad secretary is pregnant with her boss's baby, who dumped her when he found out she was pregnant, and told her to get an abortion. And when the shy editor asked her out on a date, she turned him down, so now he's sad, too."

"What a fascinating life you lead," said Harriet, a touch of mockery in her voice. She does do cynicism, and sarcasm, too, and does it well. "Full of excitement and stuff."

"It was an exciting day," Dooley confirmed, not picking up on the mockery. "Especially when Scarlett tried to teach the shy editor how to seduce a woman, and he got even more shy and all red in the face. And then there's all the scandals."

"Scandals? What scandals?" asked Harriet, her interest piqued. She does love a good scandal.

And as Dooley started listing all the trouble Advantage's CEO was facing, Brutus fell back, and gestured for me to do the same.

"I don't know what to do, Max," he told me in a low voice once we were out of Harriet's earshot.

"What do you mean?" I asked.

"Harriet wants me to be in the shoot with her. She says it's important for the contrast. She calls it the beauty and the beast effect. But I don't know. Do I really want to be the beast to her beauty? When *Cat Life* hits the stands I'm going to be the laughingstock of the whole town. They're never going to let me live it down."

"I think you'll find that these short bursts of notoriety pass very quickly," I said. "It's just one news cycle, Brutus. The next day something else pops up, and that picture will be yesterday's news, that copy of *Cat Life* used to put at the bottom of the litter box."

He gave me a look of astonishment. "My face is going to be at the bottom of a litter box?"

"At the bottom of many litter boxes all across the country, I'm sure. Or to wrap up a nice fat piece of codfish. Or even to light a fire in the stove." I gave him a pat on the shoulder. "What's more important: Harriet's face is going to serve the same purpose. So there's something to consider."

His face lit up with a smile. "I better not tell her. She'll be appalled."

"Fame is fleeting, Brutus, and so is notoriety. So I wouldn't worry about it."

"Gee, thanks, Max. You certainly put things in perspective for me."

"Glad to be of assistance, buddy. Now you be the beast to Harriet's beauty, and have fun while you're at it. It's not every day that you get to be a photo model."

I didn't want to bore him with my private thoughts about the dark clouds gathering over the Advantage Publishing Company. It just might detract from his enjoyment, and Harriet's, over being the belle of the ball for a day—or the beast.

On the other side of town, Alec Lip and Charlene Butterwick were panting heavily. They'd just tried out another tip from that *Glimmer* article '15 Ways to Spice up Your Love Life,' as written by one Tom Mitchell, and were frankly beat.

"I don't know how people do it," Alec lamented as he placed a hand on his painful back. "I think I've pulled a muscle—or ten."

"Me, too," said Charlene. She tried to move her leg and

when a spasm shot through it, winced. "This Tom Mitchell, whoever he is, must be a sadist."

"Or a masochist," Alec supplied. "One of them BDSM fanatics."

"You liked the whip, though, didn't you?"

"The whip was fine, until your secretary walked in."

"Imelda is very discreet," Charlene assured her boyfriend.

"I'll bet she is. So discreet the whole town will know about our escapades by this time tomorrow."

Charlene frowned at this piece of news. "You think?"

"Absolutely. Her best friend is Dolores Peltz, and Dolores just happens to be the precinct's biggest blabbermouth. So if she knows, everybody knows."

"Oh, let them gossip," said Charlene. "We're consenting adults, and we're doing nothing wrong."

"No, I guess not," said Alec, wiping the beads of sweat from his brow. "Still, it's going to be weird when the chief of police and the mayor are the talk of the town."

"It might help me with my ratings," said Charlene as she gingerly crawled back into bed, from where they'd fallen when practicing this latest stunt. "Ouch," she muttered when another twinge of pain shot through her leg. "I just hope I'll be able to walk tomorrow." A spicy love life was one thing, but not if it turned you into a cripple.

"I'm going to have a word with this Tom Mitchell," Alec grunted as he stretched out on the floor, hoping to give his painful back some respite.

"He probably doesn't even exist. These *Glimmer* editors all use fake names so they can avoid people complaining about the stuff they write." She glanced down at her boyfriend. "Do you want to move on to number four on the list?" But Alec gave her such a look of despair that she quickly dropped the idea. To be honest, she'd had enough herself for a while.

"How about I warm up a pancake and make us some hot chocolate?" she suggested.

"Oh, yes, please," said Alec. He tried to get up, but failed. "Maybe a little later."

They hadn't wanted to turn into a boring old couple, but sometimes you simply had to accept the naked facts: they were a boring old couple, and there was nothing wrong with that.

So she turned on Netflix, and before long they were engrossed in the latest romantic comedy, this one of Brazilian origin. Tom Mitchell might not approve, but she didn't care. By then, Alec had managed to crawl back into bed, and they watched the movie together, like the boring old people they were—and loved it.

CHAPTER 19

The next morning I woke up from an incessant ringing. At first I thought the ringing was in my ears, but when both Odelia and Chase's phones started buzzing, I finally rubbed the sleep from my eyes and paid attention.

"Your uncle," said Chase as he picked his phone from the nightstand.

"My uncle," Odelia echoed as she did the same.

Grace, meanwhile, was wailing in distress, and demanding to be picked up and fed, and since it was now obvious that no more nap time would be enjoyed, Dooley and I jumped off the bed, ready to start our day.

We were working cats now, you see, with a commute to look forward to.

But that was before we heard Chase cry, "What?!"

We both turned, and watched the big guy hop out of bed, and hurry down the stairs, still only dressed in a pair of boxers.

"What's going on?" asked Dooley.

"I have no idea," said Odelia. "Chase was first to pick up."

The ringing turned out to be the front doorbell, and when we heard Uncle Alec's baritone, it soon became clear something terrible had happened. Uncle Alec might be a fun uncle to Odelia, but he's also chief of police, and so when he shows up unannounced at some ungodly hour, he doesn't come bearing gifts.

"Michael Madison is dead," Chase announced the moment Odelia arrived downstairs.

"What?!" our human cried, echoing her husband's earlier sentiments upon hearing this piece of unexpected news.

"I'm afraid so," said Uncle Alec, looking more rumpled than ever. He was also rubbing his back and making painful grimaces as he did. "The janitor found him early this morning. Apparently he either fell or jumped out of a window."

Harriet and Brutus had walked in through the pet flap, quickly followed by Gran—the latter entering not through the pet flap but the door—and when Gran saw her granddaughter's consternation, instantly knew something was wrong.

"Who died?" she asked.

"Michael Madison," said Uncle Alec, still rubbing his back.

"What?!" Gran cried. It seemed like the response *du jour*.

"Fell out of his window," Chase supplied.

"Or jumped," Odelia added. She'd been studying her uncle with a look of concern. "Back trouble?"

"Yeah," said Uncle Alec. "I sprained something last night." And when we all lifted an inquisitive eyebrow, he elucidated, "I was, um, doing some weeding."

"Is what you kids call it nowadays?" asked Gran with a grin.

"Well, it's all your fault, isn't it!" her son suddenly burst out.

Gran held up her hands. "Easy, tiger. What's my fault this time?"

"You and that magazine of yours. *Glimmer*, or whatever it's called."

"Not my magazine, but whatever," said Gran.

"When Charlene heard you were an intern at Advantage, she took a subscription, just out of solidarity. And read an article by a guy called Tom Mitchell. 15 Ways to Spice up Your Love Life. So she's got us going through the tips one by one, which is how we both ended up almost crippling ourselves."

"Tom Mitchell didn't write that article," said Gran. "Scarlett did."

Uncle Alec groaned. "I should have known."

"And let me tell you that the response has been very positive," Gran continued. "Hundreds of comments on the website, and plenty of likes and shares."

"I'm writing a strongly-worded comment today, and I can promise you it won't be positive," the police chief grumbled as he hobbled in the direction of the door. "And you better get your ass over to that crime scene, Chase!"

"I thought it was an accident?" said Chase as he scratched his bare chest.

"Doesn't matter what it was. It's still a suspicious death, so there needs to be an investigation." And he muttered, "I'll bet Michael Madison read Tom Mitchell's article and killed himself trying out those fifteen tips."

While Chase and Odelia returned upstairs to take a shower and get ready, Harriet drew me aside. "Michael Madison is *Cat Life's* publisher, isn't he?"

"Was," I said.

"Oh, dear. Do you think my shoot will still happen? I

mean, publishers get killed all the time, don't they? And replaced by other people?"

"I'm sure your shoot will happen," I said. "Madison's death isn't going to affect that. Advantage Publishing is bigger than one CEO who falls from a window."

"Oh, phew," said Harriet. She laughed. "Talk about a load off my mind!"

"But who's going to take care of Natalie's baby now?" asked Dooley. "Her baby is going to be born without a father."

"Madison wasn't prepared to be that baby's father anyway," I told my friend. "So his death isn't going to make a lot of difference." Though Natalie would probably be devastated, considering how hung up she still was on that man.

Odelia and Chase came hurrying down the stairs, grabbed a bite to eat from the fridge, and then we were off in Chase's squad car. For the occasion, Harriet and Brutus also joined us, since Harriet wanted to make sure her shoot would go off without a hitch. And also Gran was in the car with us, for in spite of this tragic event, today was just another working day for her, same way it was for us.

When we arrived at the Advantage Publishing building, plenty of people stood gathered outside, and they weren't enjoying a smoking break either. The area underneath Michael Madison's window had been cordoned off, and I could see Abe Cornwall's car parked nearby. The county coroner was already busy examining the body, and when we joined him, he looked up.

"So what's the verdict, Abe?" asked Chase.

"He's dead," deadpanned the wiry-haired medical examiner, and got up with a slight creaking sound of the knees. "Wounds consistent with a drop from that window up there," he said, pointing to a window on the third floor. "Death would have been instantaneous."

"So what do you think happened? Was he pushed? Did he jump?"

"No defensive wounds as far as I can tell. He just fell on his head and died." He shrugged. "Nothing more to tell, really, unless you want me to get technical."

"Time of death?"

"Between two and five last night."

"I wonder if there's a camera," said Chase as he glanced around.

"There's a camera covering the parking area," said Gran. "But that's on the other side of the building. I doubt there's any cameras out here."

"No, I don't see any either," said Chase. "I'll talk to security to make sure."

And since there was nothing more for us to do out there, we moved indoors. The actual scene of the crime—if a crime had been committed, that is—was Michael Madison's office. So the small gang gathered once more there. The window was still open, but there were no signs of a struggle as far as I could tell. Crime scene people were checking the office, and one of them beckoned Chase over and showed him something on a laptop.

Chase's face hardened. "Suicide note," he told us, and read from the screen, "'I can't do this anymore. I'm sorry. Goodbye, cruel world, goodbye.' Looks like we've got a suicide on our hands, people."

"He was under a lot of pressure," Gran confirmed. "Trouble with his wife, with his mistress, personnel problems, numerous scandals." She shook her head. "It must have all gotten too much for the poor guy, so he saw no other solution."

"It's a great drop," said Harriet, who'd jumped up on that window.

"Can you please get down from there?" said Odelia, when

she saw several of Abe's CSI people freaking out at the sight of a cat jumping all over their crime scene.

"Too bad Michael Madison wasn't a cat," said Harriet as she jumped down again and joined us. "He would have landed on his feet and been just fine."

"I guess that could be said about all humans," said Brutus, the philosopher.

"When was the note written?" asked Odelia.

Chase checked the laptop. "Three o'clock."

"Consistent with Abe's time frame."

Chase nodded. "Looks like a cut-and-dried case of suicide."

An officer escorted a man into the office who was dressed in a uniform. I'd seen him hanging around the lobby the day before, keeping an eye on things.

"Detective," said the security guard, touching his cap.

"Are there any cameras covering this side of the building?" asked Chase, not wasting any time.

"There's a camera covering the fence, but it doesn't cover the back of the building," said the man.

Chase nodded. "Any cameras inside the office?"

"I'm afraid not. There's a camera in the lobby, but not in the actual offices."

The detective's eye fell on the door, which had one of those electronic locks that can only be opened with a badge. "Could you pull up the badge activity from last night? See if there was anyone else in the building apart from Madison?"

"I already checked, sir," said the security guard, "and the only badge that was used last night was Mike Madison's. He arrived early yesterday morning and never left."

"Who was the last person to leave, apart from Madison?"

"That would be Janice Wiskari, sir. She's the cleaner in charge of this floor. She left at eleven last night."

"And no one else entered?"

"No one, sir."

"So Madison was all alone in here from eleven o'clock onward, until three o'clock, when he wrote that message," Chase murmured as he fingered his chin.

"When can we allow people in, sir?" asked the security man. "It's just that they're all starting to arrive, and they're getting antsy."

Chase nodded, and walked out to confer with the security guy.

And since there was nothing further for us to do, Dooley and I wandered off, and soon found ourselves outside again, taking a closer look at that crime scene.

"Humans are fragile, aren't they, Max?" Dooley remarked. "I mean, it's not that high, and still Mr. Madison ended up dead? It's hard to imagine."

"Humans are fragile," I confirmed. "Though some have been known to survive a fall from an even greater height."

"It's true," he said. "I once saw a documentary about a woman who fell from a plane and survived. Planes fly very high in the sky, and she fell all the way down and lived. The plane did fly over a jungle, so the jungle must have broken her fall."

"Yeah, Madison had no jungle," I said, glancing at the mass of people smoking and talking and generally looking shocked—but also strangely pleased. As if this tragedy had supplied a modicum of excitement to an otherwise dull day.

Just then, I thought I saw movement in a nearby bush, and moved a little closer. And it was as I approached said bush that I saw what had caused the movement: it was a small, brown creature, with a pointy head and a round nose.

"Will you look at that," said Dooley. "It's a badger, Max."

"A badger?" I said. "What is it doing here?"

"Maybe it got lost," Dooley suggested. "Hi, there, badger," he said. "Can we help you, sir?"

"Who are you?" asked the badger, eyeing us suspiciously.

"My name is Max," I said. "And this is Dooley. We're cats."

"I know what you are," said the badger, still continuing to be suspicious.

"Do you live around here?" I asked, trying to strike up a conversation.

"What's it to you, cat?" asked the badger.

"Max," I repeated. "My name is Max. And what's yours?"

But my question was greeted with hostile silence.

"He's not going to eat us, is he?" I asked Dooley. Since my friend watches the Discovery Channel all the time, he's better placed than me to know about the habits of strange creatures like this.

"Badgers don't eat cats," said Dooley. "At least I don't think so."

"No, I don't eat cats," said the badger. "And cats don't eat badgers—or do you?"

"No, we don't eat badgers," I hastened to say.

"We're vegetarians," Dooley said with an ingratiating smile. "We only eat kibble and wet food pouches supplied by our humans. And a piece of fish from time to time. Or a piece of sausage when our humans organize a barbecue."

"You do know that your kibble and wet food and those sausages are made of meat, don't you?" said the badger.

Dooley frowned. "Pretty sure that's not the case," he said. "You see, I love all creatures great and small, and would never eat them. That's not how I roll."

"There's chicken in your kibble. Chickens are animals. So how can you call yourself a vegetarian if you eat chicken?"

"Pretty sure I don't eat chicken," Dooley insisted.

"God, you're dumb," said the badger, who wasn't the most friendly badger I'd ever encountered. Then again, he was also the first badger I ever met, so maybe all badgers were like this.

"I'm not dumb," said Dooley kindly. "I'm a vegetarian."

Suddenly I got an idea. "You didn't happen to see a guy fall out of a window last night, did you?" I asked, gesturing in the direction of the nearby building.

"Sure," said the badger, much to my surprise. "Though he didn't actually fall from that window."

"What do you mean?" I asked, experiencing that tingle in my tail I get when a case suddenly presents itself to me.

"I mean he was pushed."

"Pushed? You mean pushed by some other person?"

"He wasn't pushed by a badger, if that's what you mean," said the badger with a touch of acerbity. "Yeah, pushed by another person. Plenty of screaming and shouting, too. Which is how I came to pop up from my burrow to take a look. I was just in time to see one person shove another person out of that window over there. And if that wasn't enough, the person doing the shoving came out of the building a couple of minutes later, to check on the guy he dropped."

"To see if he was still alive, you mean?"

The badger nodded. "Checked his pulse and then skedaddled."

"Did you see this person's face?" I asked, excitement making my heart race.

"Nah. He was wearing one of them black masks."

"He? So it was a man?"

"When I say 'he' I don't actually mean 'he,' you see. It could have been a she."

"I see. And you're absolutely positive about this?"

"Do I look like the kind of badger who would make up a story like that?"

"No, I guess not," I admitted. He certainly didn't look like the flaky type.

"Okay, so if there's nothing else, I think I'll take a hike

now," said the badger. "Badgers to see and things to do and all that." And before we could stop him, he had disappeared into a hole in the ground.

"Hey, you haven't told us your name!" I yelled after him.

But he was gone, with my voice echoing along the walls of the hole he'd dug.

"That's a burrow," said Dooley as he studied the hole. "Also called a den or a sett. Badgers are great diggers. That's what they do. They dig. They use these dens to sleep during the day, and then they hunt during the night. Which is why he was up and about to watch Michael Madison fall out of his office window."

"Or being pushed," I said. "By a mystery person with a black mask."

Dooley stared at me, dismay written all over his face. "So… he was murdered?"

I nodded thoughtfully. "That's certainly what it looks like, Dooley."

"Oh, dear. That's not very nice."

CHAPTER 20

We were all gathered in Uncle Alec's office. I'd told Odelia that a credible witness had confirmed Madison was murdered, which put a completely different spin on things.

"It's tough," said the chief of police as he placed two beefy arms on his desk blotter. "A badger is not a good witness. A judge is not going to accept his statement. And neither is a cat. So frankly we got nothing."

"We know it was murder," Odelia argued.

"I know we know it was murder. But not officially we don't. Not with a badger as a witness." He frowned darkly in my direction, as if I was personally to blame for this dilemma.

"But we have to investigate," said Chase. "If the guy was murdered, there has to be a murder investigation."

"You know as well as I do that there needs to be a reasonable suspicion. What am I going to tell the DA? That a badger talked to my niece's cat, who told my niece, who told me? He's going to lock me up in the loony bin and throw away the key." He shook his head. "No, we have to tackle this thing differently. We need to approach this from a different angle. An angle that leaves us out of it entirely."

"And with us you mean the police," said Chase.

Uncle Alec eyed his niece keenly. "You're going to tell people you're working for Madison's insurance company. Investigating a life insurance claim."

"That might be difficult," said Odelia. "Since a lot of these people know me as a reporter for the *Gazette*."

"You could them you're moonlighting as an insurance investigator?" But when Odelia gave him a look that said, 'Are you kidding me?' he relented. "Yeah I guess that wouldn't fly. So what do you suggest?"

Odelia shrugged. "I'm a reporter, so why not use that as my cover?"

"Excellent thinking," said her uncle, pointing a stubby finger in her direction.

"And since Gran and Scarlett are already undercover," Odelia said, "we should be able to cover all of our bases."

Her uncle rubbed his face. "I hope they don't mess it up, like they usually do."

"And what do you want me to do?" asked Chase.

"You're going to coordinate the investigation, check alibis, ask around."

"But not officially."

Uncle Alec shrugged. "Just tying up loose ends. You know the drill."

"Absolutely, Chief," said Chase.

"So there's going to be an investigation, only there's not going to be an investigation," Odelia summed things up.

"Exactly," said the Chief. "And I hope this thing won't come back to bite me in the ass. So the sooner you can crack this case and find me Madison's killer, the better, you hear? Before people start asking questions, and the DA starts breathing down my neck or, God forbid, the Mayor."

"I thought the Mayor was Uncle Alec's girlfriend?" asked Dooley.

"She is, but she's also his boss." When Dooley stared at me, I added, "It's complicated."

"Human affairs always are," he said, and not unjustly so.

"One thing I don't understand," said Chase, "is how the killer got in and out of the building without using a badge. Security is absolutely sure only Madison was in the building last night. So how did the killer move around undetected?"

"One of the mysteries you will have to solve, Max," said Odelia.

"I know what's going on," said Dooley. "He's the Invisible Man!"

"Unlikely," I said with a smile. It was a real mystery, though.

How do you move around a building where every door is locked, and can only be opened with a personalized badge connected to the security system?

It was also the topic of conversation when we met up with Gran and Scarlett in a coffee shop around the corner from the police station. Odelia and Chase were there to brief the two older ladies on their new mission: to catch Michael Madison's killer.

"So what can you tell me about potential suspects?" asked Odelia, her hand poised over her tablet.

"Oh, there's plenty," said Scarlett. "Take your pick."

"There's Tom Mitchell," said Gran, earning herself an astonished look from Scarlett. "The kid is head over heels in love with Natalie, who is expecting Madison's baby. So obviously Tom is the first suspect that comes to mind."

"Yeah, I guess so," said Scarlett reluctantly. "He's so nice, though. I don't think he's a killer."

"He could be nice and a killer," said Gran.

"So Tom Mitchell," said Odelia. "Who else?"

"Well, there's Deith Madison," said Scarlett. "We saw her storm in and out of her husband's office yesterday, and there were a lot of harsh words spoken. So if I were you I'd have a long talk with her, cause that couple was not on good terms."

"And then there's Gary Rapp," said Gran.

"Who's he?"

"Fashion editor who was fired for harassing his models. He's suing the company for wrongful termination, though there's plenty of models who filed a complaint against him with HR."

"Okay, so Gary Rapp. Upset with Madison after being fired," said Odelia, writing all this down in her neat handwriting. "Did he have a badge to the building?" she asked, then reconsidered. "Never mind. Chase will find out. Next?"

"Next is Ona Konpacka," said Scarlett, sharing a glance with Gran. "She's a model who was permanently disfigured by the plastic surgeon Madison set her up with. The poor girl is a recluse now, and is also suing Madison and Advantage Publishing for damages."

"And emotional cruelty," Gran added. "After Madison terminated her contract," she explained when Odelia looked at her expectantly.

"Okay, so we've got Tom Mitchell, Deith Madison, Gary Rapp, Ona Konpacka..."

"Let's not forget about Doris Booth," said Gran. "She was a publicist who quit her job when Madison gifted her a copy of *Elements of Style*, insinuating she couldn't spell and was unfit for her job. She wrote a letter to Dear Gabi," she explained, "but had already quit her job when we got there."

"So we never got to talk to her," said Scarlett.

"And a good thing, too," said Gran. "We've had plenty to work with trying to match up Tom and Natalie."

"You're not still going to continue that matchmaking business, are you?" said Chase. "Not when a murder has been committed?"

"We could do both," said Scarlett. "Solve Madison's murder and get Tom and Natalie together."

"It's going to be a lot easier now that Madison is gone," added Gran.

"Cold, Gran," said Odelia. "Very cold."

"I'm just being realistic!" Gran cried. She took a sip from her hot cocoa. "Okay, so who else is there? Oh, that's right. Wayne Piscina!"

"Who's Wayne Piscina?" asked Chase, who'd also been jotting down notes.

"He's an assistant who got fired for some old homophobic and racist tweets," said Scarlett. "And if I'm not mistaken, he's also suing Madison and Advantage."

"With so many people hating on Madison, it's a miracle the man survived for so long," Chase grunted as he wrote down Wayne's name. "Anyone else?"

"That's about it, I guess?" said Scarlett, looking to her friend for confirmation.

"Yeah, for now," said Gran. "Isn't that enough to get you started?"

"More than enough," Odelia agreed. "And you'll continue to dig around?"

"Oh, trust me, honey," said Scarlett. "We're going to dig like we've never dug before!"

"Funny, isn't it, Max?" said Dooley.

"What is?"

"We're all going to dig, just like that badger."

"I know. And let's hope we dig up something good."

CHAPTER 21

"I've got one more suspect," said Gran, once Dooley and I were installed in our old position on top of her desk at Advantage Publishing. "Natalie."

"You can't possibly think that poor girl had anything to do with Madison's murder," said Scarlett.

"She is pregnant with his baby, and he did treat her terribly. Telling her to get an abortion and breaking up with her. People have been murdered for less than what he did to that 'poor girl,'" Gran insisted.

"Long list of suspects," said Scarlett.

"I'm sure it's just the tip of the iceberg. Guys like Madison create lots of enemies."

"I can't believe Natalie would do a thing like that, though, or Tom. They're such a cute couple."

"They're not a couple yet, honey." She frowned. "You don't think…"

"What?"

"That they did this together, do you?"

"Are you crazy? They're hardly on speaking terms."

"Mh. I guess you're right," said Gran, then sighed. "Oh,

well. Looks like we've got a couple to unite, *and* a murder to solve. No pressure!"

"I wonder if there could have been a ladder," I told Dooley.

"A ladder?"

"Yeah, if the murderer got in through Madison's window by putting a ladder up against the building."

"The badger didn't mention a ladder."

"We didn't ask."

"If there was a ladder, he would have mentioned it."

"Maybe not. Maybe badgers don't think anything about ladders set up against buildings and used to murder people. Maybe they think it's just par for the course."

We both thought about this for a moment, and soon came to the same conclusion: we had to talk to that badger again. Which was going to prove hard, since he had disappeared down his burrow—or den or sett.

In the meantime Gran had taken it upon herself to talk to Natalie again, and try to find out about her involvement with the death of her boss.

※

"You're kidding," said Natalie, as she stared, wide-eyed, at Vesta.

"No, I'm not," said Vesta as she shoved a cup underneath that recalcitrant coffee machine she'd been struggling with since the day she arrived at Advantage. "The police think Madison might have been pushed."

"But I heard they found a suicide note?"

"Suicide notes can be faked."

"Oh, God. This just keeps getting worse and worse!" the glorified secretary said, clutching a distraught hand to her face. She looked pale and drawn, which was no surprise. The man she professed to love had just been killed, and yet here she was, still showing up for work.

"If I were you I'd go home," Vesta now told the girl. "There's nothing you can do here."

"I can't go home," said Natalie.

"Your brother still giving you a hard time?"

Natalie nodded. "We had a flaming row last night. When I arrived the place was a mess. He'd invited a couple of his friends and they'd spilled cigarette ashes all over my furniture, slices of pizza left upside down on my coffee table, beer soaked into my carpets. You should have seen the place, Vesta. It was such a mess. So I threw them all out and told Luke to clean up, which he refused."

"I think you should kick him out."

"I would, but he's got nowhere else to stay."

"He's got friends. He can bunk with them." And mess up their places.

"I couldn't do that to him. He's still my brother." She sighed. "Before mom died, I promised I'd always take care of my little brother, and I won't break that promise."

"You know what I think? Luke knows you made that promise, and now he's taking advantage of you."

"I know," said Natalie miserably. "And now with Madison gone, I don't know what to do."

"You're still having the baby?"

The girl nodded wordlessly.

"Even though its dad is dead?"

At the sound of those awful words, Natalie burst into tears. Vesta handed her a tissue, which she used to dry her eyes and blow her nose. "It's all just so terrible," she said. "My baby is going to grow up without a daddy."

"From what I understand, your baby was going to grow up without a daddy, whether Madison had lived or not."

"I know this is stupid of me... but I was still hoping for a reconciliation, you know. Michael once told me he loved me. And a love like that—it can't just go away, can it?"

It can if it was never there in the first place, Vesta thought. "I'm sure everything will be all right," she assured the young woman as she patted her back consolingly. And as they walked back to the office, she asked, "Could you think of anyone who would hurt Michael, Natalie?"

"No one," she said immediately. "The man was a saint. When you look at the kind of stuff he had to put up with every day—the man was an absolute saint."

"Of course he was. A regular saint."

※

Scarlett wanted to talk to Tom, with whom she felt she had built up a nice rapport the day before, but unfortunately he wasn't at his desk. And when she asked his cousin Danny, he told her Tom was taking a sick day.

"He wasn't feeling well this morning," Danny said as he took a seat on the edge of her desk. "So I told him to stay in bed. And a good thing I did, considering what happened with Madison."

"I thought Tom didn't like Madison?"

"Who did? But he's got enough to deal with right now, without having to look at Natalie crying her heart out because her precious boyfriend dropped dead last night."

Natalie was back at her desk, and from the quaking motion of her shoulders, it was obvious she was going through yet another box of Kleenex.

"He took Natalie's rejection pretty hard," Danny said. "After he screwed up his courage like that, and finally popped the question, the way she turned him down flat—that was cold, Scarlett. That was cold of her." He directed an equally icy look at Natalie's back, clearly unhappy with the way the girl had treated his cousin. "I keep telling him to forget about her. There's plenty of fish in the sea, right?"

"Plenty," Scarlett confirmed, who knew from experience this was true.

"But no. He keeps insisting Natalie is the only one for him. The idiot."

"Did you tell Tom about what happened to Madison?" asked Scarlett.

"I sent him a text."

"And?"

"He's shocked, of course. Just like we all are. I mean, I always thought Madison was hard as nails. The toughest boss I ever worked for. But turns out the man was fighting some inner demons that none of us knew about. And then he goes and kills himself. Just goes to show you never really know a person, do you?"

"No, I guess you don't," said Scarlett, darting a glance at Madison's empty office, which was sealed off by police tape.

"So you and Tom were home last night, were you? Didn't go out?"

He gave her an odd look, then nodded. "Of course. Where would we go?"

"I don't know. Out. Couple of young guys like you? Hitting the town hard?"

"Tom isn't one for hitting the town hard, especially in the state he's been in. And I may not look it, but I'm a homebody at heart. And besides, my aunt likes us all home safe and sound with her. She's old-fashioned like that."

Scarlett made a mental note for Odelia to check with Tom's mom if she could confirm Tom's alibi, but she had no reason to doubt Danny's words. Tom may have been upset with Madison for the way he was treating Natalie, but the soft-spoken young man didn't strike her as a cold-blooded killer.

And that this was cold-blooded murder was clear. Someone had taken great pains to make Madison's death look like a suicide, and had planned this well, even making sure he or she weren't detected by the building's security system.

"Thanks, Danny," she said. "And when you hear from Tom, give him my love, will you?"

"Will do," said Danny, and was on his way again, pushing his cart.

The big boss might be dead, but life at Advantage went on. Soon corporate would put a new boss in charge, who would move into Madison's office, and Madison's death would be a minor blip on the radar of this multi-million-dollar business empire.

CHAPTER 22

Looked like it wasn't business as usual at Advantage after all, for around eleven a representative of management showed up, and told everyone to go home. In light of the circumstances, they had reached the decision that we couldn't very well be expected to give of our best, and so we were all asked to leave, and Advantage Publishing was closing down for the time being.

"When are they going to reopen again?" asked Gran as we stepped into the elevator.

"No idea," said Natalie, pressing a Kleenex to her nose. "I think it's very decent of them, don't you? To give us time to grieve?"

"Yes, very decent," said Gran, though I didn't think she meant it.

"It's the stock," Danny explained, offering a less roseate view of management. "It's dropping like a rock. If this keeps up there won't be any shareholders left."

Natalie's eyes widened. "Dropping like a rock because…"

"Because of what happened to Madison," Danny confirmed. "You can't have a CEO of a company jumping out of his office window and not expect an effect on the price of the company's shares. People are unloading Advantage stock as fast as they can, and management is probably freaking out, wondering how they're going to stop the bleed." He cursed under his breath. "And to think we all got stock options. If this keeps up they'll be completely worthless."

"I don't have stock options," said Natalie.

"What do you mean? We all got them when we started. It's in your contract."

"It is?" said Natalie, who clearly wasn't *au courant* with her compensation plan.

"You should talk to HR," Danny advised. "Though now that the stock is in the toilet, maybe better don't. It will only depress you."

And so we found ourselves out on the street again.

"Well, it was great while it lasted," said Gran as we sauntered in the direction of the car. I was still on the lookout for that badger, but I couldn't see him.

"We'll be back," Scarlett assured her friend.

"You think? I'll bet they'll restructure the company, redesign the office, hire a new CEO, and this entire senior intern scheme will go right out the window."

"Just like Madison," said Dooley cheerfully, earning himself a grin from Gran.

"So how are we going to assist Odelia with her investigation now?" asked Scarlett.

"I don't know, honey. I guess we'll just have to wait and see what happens."

And after directing a final glance at the building we got to call home for the past two days, we all got into Gran's battered red Peugeot.

"Can you just hang on for a second?" I asked.

"Sure," said Gran. "But make it fast, will you?"

"Where is he off to?" asked Scarlett.

"My guess is either wee-wee or doo-doo," said Gran.

Dooley hurried to keep up with me. "So what is it, Max? Wee-wee or doo-doo?"

"Neither," I said curtly. "I want to take one last shot at that badger."

"You want to shoot the badger?" he asked, shocked. "But why?"

"I'm not going to shoot the badger, Dooley. I just want to talk to him."

We arrived at that bush, and hunkered down at the edge of the burrow. "Hey, Mr. Badger!" Dooley cried. "Max has another question for you, sir!"

We waited for a moment, but when no response was forthcoming, I said, "Looks like we'll have to do this the hard way." And so I headed into the hole.

Before you draw the wrong conclusion, let me assure you that I'm no hero. I'm not some Dirty Harry or John Wayne who goes off to fight the good fight, guns blazing. But I needed to know about that ladder, and since the badger was the only witness we had, I saw no other recourse than to find him where he was hiding.

"Max! Come back!" Dooley cried.

But I just kept on burrowing down into that burrow.

If my calculations were correct, this was just a short pipe, which would end in a larger underground dug-out hollow, where Mr. Badger was taking a nap, since badgers hunt at night and sleep during the day, as Dooley had explained.

"Max!" Dooley yelled. "These tunnels can run thirty feet deep!"

Yikes! Now if I'd known that...

Unfortunately there was no way for me to turn around, so the only thing I could do was keep going!

Lucky for me, this particular badger must have been a lazy badger, for it only took me about ten feet to reach a larger cavern, and lo and behold: the badger was indeed taking a well-deserved nap... along with three more badgers!

To say my arrival was greeted with general confusion and upheaval is an understatement.

"Intruder!" one of the badgers screamed, causing the other badgers to wake up, and strike a defensive pose, which consisted of their forearms going up. And when you know that a badger has some very powerful and muscular forearms, you can imagine that I was having second thoughts about my rash initiative!

"I come in peace!" I quickly assured them. "Now which one of you is the badger I talked to before?"

"That would be me," said the biggest badger in the room.

"Oh, hi," I said, injecting as much warmth and reassurance into my voice as possible. "And is this Mrs. Badger and kids? So nice to meet you, one and all."

"What do you want?" the badger grunted, clearly not one for small talk.

"Don't be rude, Richard," said the lady badger. "Is this how you welcome visitors into our home? Don't mind my husband, sir," she said. "He's not usually this blunt. He's got a toothache is all, and it's affecting his mood."

"You've got a toothache?" I said. "It's just that I know a great veterinarian. She helped me get rid of a toothache not so long ago. If you want, I could introduce you."

"Just ask the question," the badger said.

But before I could, there was a sort of commotion behind me, and Dooley dropped in!

"Another intruder!" the same small badger yelled.

"It's my friend Dooley," I quickly explained.

"Oh, this is cozy," said Dooley, dusting himself off.

"Well, hi there, Dooley," said Mrs. Badger. "Welcome to

our humble home. Richard?" she urged. "What do we say to our guests?"

"Welcome to our humble abode," the badger grumbled unhappily.

"And now once again, but this time with feeling."

"Look, this is wholly unnecessary," I said. "All I want to know is whether you saw a ladder parked against the building last night. When the guy fell from that window?"

"Was pushed, you mean," Richard grunted.

"Oh, that's right. You saw a man getting pushed out of a window last night, didn't you, darling?" said Mrs. Badger. "My name is Irene, by the way," she said with a kindly smile in our direction. "And these two rascals are Bert and Ernie."

"Bert and Ernie?" I asked. Somehow the names reminded me of something, though for the life of me, I couldn't remember what. It'd come to me later.

"Say hi to the nice cats, children," said Irene.

"Hi, cats!" said Bert and Ernie. The latter turned to his mom. "So they're not intruders?"

"No, they're guests."

"Uninvited guests, but whatever," Richard grumbled.

"Do you want a bite to eat?" asked Irene. "We've got some nice fat earthworms."

"No, please," I said when I spotted said worms, wriggling and squirming in a corner of the burrow. "We've already eaten. And anyway, we can't stay."

"And we're vegetarians," Dooley explained. "So we can't eat worms."

Richard rolled his eyes at this, and to avoid getting bogged down again in a discussion on what constitutes a real vegetarian, I repeated my earlier question: "So did you see a ladder planted against that building last night, Richard?"

"No, Max, I did not," said Richard, as eager to get rid of us as I was to get out of there.

"No ladder?" I asked, not hiding my disappointment.

"What's with the ladder?" asked Irene.

"No, it's just that Michael Madison, the guy who runs Advantage Publishing, was killed last night, but the only person who was in the building, at least according to the security system, was the victim. So I figured the killer must have entered the building through one of the windows, and headed straight into Madison's office, got into a fight with the guy, and shoved him out the window."

"I told you, no ladder," Richard said, fixing me with an intent look.

"Gotcha," I said. "And no distinguishing features that could identify the killer?"

"No distinguishing features," Richard said. Clearly he wanted us gone.

"Okay, I guess that's that," I said. I turned to the badger's wife. "Well, thank you so much for your hospitality, Irene, but I'm afraid we have to leave."

"So soon? How about a nice grub? They're very tasty, you know."

I threw up in my mouth a little, but I think I managed to hide it well. Until I saw a sly smile slide up Richard's face.

"Yeah, why don't you stay for dinner?" he said. "We've got some nice slugs."

"Very slimy!" said Bert.

"Very yummy!" said Ernie.

"No, that's all right," I said, having trouble keeping my stomach under control.

Dooley was making retching noises next to me, which didn't help.

"Or how about a big fat lizard?" Richard suggested.

"Gotta go," I said, retching a little. "Thanks for everything, Irene!"

"Now see what you did, Richard?" I heard Irene tell her

husband once we'd turned tail and were crawling out of that burrow again, in a hurry to reach the surface. "The one time we have guests, and you go and scare them away."

"I didn't scare them away. I offered them our best grub!"

"Oh, Richard. What am I going to do with you?"

"I don't mind!" Bert said. "It means there's more for us!"

Now that's the spirit, I thought as I dug like I'd never dug before!

And soon we reached the surface, and took in big gulps of fresh air.

"There's a reason cats aren't badgers," said Dooley, who looked a little green around the gills. "I never knew what it was before, but now I do. It's very claustrophobic to be a badger, Max!"

"Yeah, and then there's the diet," I said, panting from the exertion.

But at least I had my answer: however the killer had entered the building, it hadn't been by using a ladder. Of course this only added to the mystery.

So how had this person managed to get in and out of Madison's office?

CHAPTER 23

Odelia had arranged to meet Gary Rapp at the Steamy Bean, a sidewalk café that had proven very popular in recent months. It offered a nice view up and down Main Street, and was packed when we arrived, both with locals and tourists. Mr. Rapp was a local though, since he'd worked at Advantage Publishing for quite some time as one of *Glimmer's* more prominent fashion editors.

Until his services were no longer required, that is.

"Mrs. Kingsley," said Rapp, as he got up to welcome our human with an unctuous smile. "So nice to meet a colleague. And can I say that your reputation precedes you? Your articles are always the first ones I read every week."

"Thanks," said Odelia as she took a seat. When the server came she ordered a soda, and Rapp ordered another alcoholic beverage.

"Who is this guy?" asked Dooley.

"Gary Rapp," I said. "Disgraced former fashion editor."

"Oh, right," said Dooley, though it was obvious he still had no clue who the guy was. It was hard to keep track of the number of people Madison had crossed.

"I guess you heard what happened to Michael Madison, your former boss?" said Odelia.

"Yeah, I was shocked when I heard the news," said Rapp, shaking his head. "Such a tragic story. Mind you, Mike had been under a lot of pressure lately, and the last time I saw him I could tell he wasn't coping well. But still—to end his life like that. I already reached out to Deith, of course, to pay my respects. She's heartbroken, as you can imagine."

"I'm seeing her later," said Odelia. "First I thought I'd talk to some of the people who knew Michael well. Though from what I heard your relationship with him got a little heated in recent days? Is that correct?"

"We didn't part on amicable terms," Rapp confirmed as he fingered his drink. "Some wicked gossip poisoned Mike's mind against me, and he felt pressured into terminating my contract. I was fighting them in court, of course."

"So the rumors about harassment aren't true?" asked Odelia.

"Absolutely not!" said Rapp, looking thoroughly shocked. "I've always treated everyone with the utmost respect, and don't let anyone tell you differently. But when you've got a high-profile position, like I had, you're bound to attract all kinds of nasty gossip. And sometimes they'll go after you if they feel slighted."

"These models who accused you, they felt slighted, you think?"

"Absolutely. Not being given the cover of the magazine, for instance, or not enough coverage. That would be enough for some of these people to go after me."

"Did you blame Michael Madison for your dismissal, Gary?"

"Of course not. I knew he felt cornered by these people and their lawyers. If he didn't get rid of me they were going to tar him with the same brush. So he had no other recourse but to do what he did." He took a big swig from his drink. "No, I never blamed Mike personally. He was my friend. Though it's true he could have showed more backbone when push came to shove. He caved immediately. Which surprised me."

"You felt betrayed by your friend?"

He gave her a keen look and smiled. It was a charming smile, and I could tell that he was probably popular with the ladies. "I see what you're trying to do, Mrs. Kingsley, and it won't work. Yes, I was surprised when he called me into his office and told me he had to let me go. And yes, I argued my case—fiercely. But since then I've been doing a lot of thinking, and soul-searching, and I can honestly say I've made peace with what happened. It wasn't Mike's fault, and hey—" He spread his arms. "I'm still here. Other opportunities await. So it's all good."

Odelia shifted in her chair. "Rumor has it that Mike's death wasn't accidental."

He stared at her, visibly startled. "Not accidental? What do you mean?"

"There's a possibility that he didn't jump, but was pushed."

His eyes had gone wide. "Pushed? You mean... murder?"

Odelia nodded. "This is not official, mind you."

"Oh, my God," said the former editor.

She eyed him closely. "Can you tell me where you were last night, Gary?"

He blinked a couple of times. "You're not seriously accusing me of murder, are you?"

"No, of course not. Just doing my job. Asking questions and trying to find some answers."

"But..." He glanced around. "You're not here on police business, are you? I mean, I've heard that you work with your husband as a police consultant."

"No, this isn't one of those occasions," Odelia assured him. "I'm strictly here as a reporter for the *Gazette*. In fact as far as I know, the police are working on the assumption that this was suicide. At least that's what my sources are telling me."

"Your sources are impeccable," said Rapp, searching Odelia's face. "Your husband is a detective and your uncle is the chief of police."

"True," she admitted. "But like I said, I don't represent the police right now."

The guy seemed to relax a little. "Okay, so I want it on the record that I vehemently deny any involvement in any murder business. I liked Mike. We were friends for a long time. And I didn't hold any grudge against him. He did what he had to do as the company's CEO, and I understood and respected his decision."

"That said, can you tell me where you were last night?" Odelia insisted.

"Of course. I was at the Pussy Wagon, for the birthday party of one of the hostesses. I stayed late, until maybe, oh, three o'clock? Ask anyone. They'll confirm my alibi." He produced a wry smile. "Am I glad that I accepted that invitation last night. I didn't want to go—not in the mood—but good thing I did."

"Can you think of anyone who would want to harm Mike Madison?"

Rapp furrowed his brow and rubbed his temple. "Um… I know there was some trouble with Howard White."

"The designer?"

Rapp nodded. "*Glimmer* published a pretty scathing article on his latest collection, and Howard wasn't happy about it. Accused us of writing a hit piece."

"Who wrote the article?"

"Well, that's the interesting part. Mike wrote it himself.

Before he became CEO he was a pretty accomplished editor himself, and he liked to keep his hand in, so to speak. At first Howard thought I'd written the piece, so he came after me. But Mike was decent enough to own up and admit he was the actual culprit."

"And Howard wasn't happy with Mike."

"You can say that again. They had a flaming row in Mike's office."

"When was this?"

"Couple of days ago. I wasn't there, of course, but a friend texted me. Said it was epic." He flashed a quick grin. "Howard really threw his weight around."

Odelia nodded and wrote down the name. "Anyone else?"

Rapp shook his head slowly. "Not that I can think of. I mean, how sure are you that it was murder? Who is your source?"

She smiled. "You know I can't tell you, Gary. Let's just say I'm pretty sure."

"God. Who would do such a thing? It's just so..." He lapsed into silence, then dumped the remainder of his drink down the hatch in one go. "So *barbaric*."

CHAPTER 24

It wasn't easy for Odelia to arrange an interview with Ona Konpacka. The former model wasn't giving interviews—no exceptions. In fact according to her former publicist she wasn't seeing anyone, a big change from before, when she had enjoyed a dozen *Glimmer* covers—the most for any model ever—and her face had featured on anything from billboards to commercials to cameos in blockbuster movies. But no more.

If Miss Konpacka thought Odelia would give up so easily, she was mistaken, though. She can be quite tenacious, our human. And so instead of going in herself, she dispatched Dooley and me to do the honors. Yikes!

"I've never done an interview for the *Gazette* before, Max," said Dooley nervously. "I'm not sure I can do it. We haven't had the training!"

"We're not actually going to interview Miss Konpacka," I told him. "We're just going to talk to her miniature Brussels Griffon Joey."

"What's a Brussels Griffon, Max? Is that like a Brussels sprout?"

"I doubt it, Dooley," I said. "I think it's hard to interview a Brussels sprout."

Odelia had dropped us off in front of the apartment building where Ona Konpacka lived. According to her information—gleaned from Gran and Scarlett—the prematurely retired supermodel adored her Brussels Griffon Joey, and allowed no one else close to her accept the tiny doggie, who had been her constant companion when she was still traveling the world to the most exotic locations on the planet for her photoshoots, and who was her only friend now.

"Toi toi toi!" Odelia said as she watched us mount the fire escape that snaked up the tall brown brick building.

"Why does Odelia call us Toi?" asked Dooley.

"It's an expression people use to wish someone luck," I explained. "Like break a leg?"

Dooley started violently. "But I don't want to break a leg!"

"If you tell someone to break a leg, they're not going to break a leg," I said. "It's a kind of superstition."

"I see," he said, but I could see that he didn't.

We climbed that fire escape to the top floor, where the model lived, and I sincerely hoped that Odelia had done her homework, and Ona hadn't traded in her miniature Brussels Griffon with a Doberman. Or a pit bull terrier! Cats may be brave creatures, always ready to dive into a badger's burrow, but we're not suicidal!

"I wonder what Harriet and Brutus are up to," said Dooley. "And why they're not here with us right now. I mean, I don't mind being Odelia's eyes and ears, but it's always the same cats having to do her dirty work, isn't it, Max?"

"It's because she trusts us, Dooley," I said.

"You mean she doesn't trust Harriet and Brutus?"

I hesitated. "I wouldn't go as far as that," I said, prevaricating. "But maybe she trusts us just that little bit more than she does our friends. And anyway, Harriet is too busy preserving her beauty and worrying about her shoot right now, and Brutus has to make sure she looks her absolute best all the time, so there's that."

"I wouldn't mind being on the cover of *Cat Life*. I may not be the prettiest cat around, but I'm not that ugly either, right?"

"No, you're not ugly at all," I said with a smile.

"Or maybe you could be on the cover, Max. I'm sure in this day and age of diversity, a plus-sized model like you would look good on the cover of *Cat Life*."

My smile vanished. "Let's just focus on the task at hand, shall we?" I suggested. All this talk about cover models was starting to annoy me. We had a murder to solve, after all, not contemplate ways and means of making *Cat Life* more diverse.

We finally arrived on the balcony that wrapped around Ona Konpacka's apartment, and took a moment to catch our breath. When I looked down, I could see Odelia leaning against her pickup, patiently awaiting our return, hopefully with some exciting news about this potential suspect.

We didn't have long to search for the model's constant companion: on the other side of the glass window a little doggie was staring back at us. It looked like one of the Ewoks in those Star Wars movies: very tiny and very hairy.

"It looks like a rat," said Dooley when he caught sight of the creature.

"I'm sure it's not a rat," I assured him.

"Or a badger."

The doggie, recovering from the shock of this sudden and unexpected intrusion, started barking furiously, jerking back and forth as it did in a sort of full-body spasm. For a moment I thought it was going to have a heart attack, but it seemed to be the way it responded to unwanted intruders.

After what felt like an eternity, a human person appeared,

and when I looked up, I found myself gazing into the face that had once been described by an astute observer as the most beautiful face in the world.

Now I'm not a human myself, of course, so I'm not exactly the best judge of what constitutes or doesn't constitute beauty in humans, but this particular face didn't exactly strike me as particularly beautiful. Then again, tastes differ.

Ona Konpacka, if this was her, had a sort of square face, with plenty of lumps where no lumps were supposed to be, and lips that were entirely too plump for comfort. In fact her face looked like a landscape, but with the dales and peaks in all the wrong places. Possibly a consequence of that botched cosmetic procedure.

She frowned at us a good deal, picking up Joey in the process, then finally opened the sliding glass door to take a closer look at this oddly mismatched duo.

"Did you guys get lost?" she asked. "You climbed and climbed and now you don't know how to get down?"

As agreed, both Dooley and I started meowing piteously, clawing the air with one paw, and making the kind of pleading faces humans think only dogs can make. It prompted the kind of response we were hoping for: Ona Konpacka's cat eyes—perhaps the result of one too many facelifts—turned moist with pity.

"Oh, will you look at these two sweeties!" she cried, as she bent down. In the process the Ewok poured from her arms and took up its barking frenzy once more. "No, Joey," said Ona sternly. "Can't you see you're scaring the poor kitties?"

"Yeah, you're scaring the poor kitties, Joey," said Dooley.

The doggie abruptly stopped barking. "Who are you?" it demanded.

"My name is Max," I said. "And this is my friend Dooley."

"I'll go and get you something to eat," Ona announced,

and wagged a warning finger at Joey. "There will be no more barking, you hear? Be nice to the kitties."

"Yes, be nice to the kitties," Dooley echoed.

Ona returned indoors, and then it was just us and Joey.

"So are you a girl or a boy?" asked Dooley, curious. "Or neither?"

"How can I be neither?" said Joey, plunking down on its tush.

"We met a person in Paris who was neither a boy or a girl," Dooley explained.

"Well, if you must know, I'm a girl," said Joey. "Though I'm not sure if it's any of your business." She was still eyeing us with distinct hostility, so I felt we needed to address the situation if we were to make any progress here today.

"Look, we're not here to stay," I told her. "Or to invade your space. We're here because a man died last night, and we think he was murdered. And now we're trying to figure out who could have murdered him. And since your human knew this man, we wanted to have a chat and see what she knows."

Joey gave me a look of surprise. "Someone was murdered? Who?"

"Michael Madison," I said. "The publisher of *Glimmer* magazine?"

"I know *Glimmer*," said Joey. "Ona used to work for them a lot."

"She was on the cover twelve times!" said Dooley, who'd listened carefully when Odelia had given us our brief for this interview. "The most times any model was featured on *Glimmer*—ever."

"And Ona kept every single cover, framed on the wall of her study." Then Joey's furry little face sagged. "Or at least she used to. Now they're all packed up in a crate somewhere, locked up in storage—probably forever. She removed every single photograph of herself and every single mirror from the apartment after…"

"After the incident," I said, nodding.

Joey glanced over her shoulder. "It was a sad day when it happened, and Ona still hasn't recovered. We used to travel the globe, you know, she and I. One week we were in Thailand for a shoot on the beach, the next in Paris for a shoot with the Eiffel Tower as backdrop, or Bermuda or Senegal or Switzerland. It was a jet-setting life and all great fun… As long as it lasted."

"She doesn't leave the apartment anymore?"

"Hasn't set foot outside since… the incident."

"Doesn't eat out? Doesn't receive visitors?"

"Nothing. No one is allowed, not even her siblings or her mom and dad. She doesn't want to see anyone—or anyone seeing her. Even the kid who delivers her meals isn't allowed to see her. He leaves the box in the hall, and she won't come out until he's gone. It's a sad, sad life, Max and Dooley. And very, very lonely." She gave us a weak smile, and for the first time I sensed the little doggie's loneliness.

"So maybe she should get you a companion?" Dooley suggested. "A Brussels sprout, maybe?"

"A Brussels sprout is a vegetable, Dooley," I explained.

"Oh, so maybe a Paris Griffon? Or a London Griffon?"

"Forgive my friend," I told Joey. "He's just trying to be helpful."

"I know," said Joey. "And I appreciate it. I've told Ona a million times to find me a friend, but unfortunately she doesn't speak our language."

"Maybe we could tell Odelia," Dooley suggested. "And she could tell Ona."

"Who's Odelia?"

"Our human," I explained. "And she does speak our language."

"Oh, if you could do that for me?" said Joey, her eyes lighting up. "I've been dreaming about having some company for so long. It would be like a dream come true. I mean, don't get me wrong—I adore Ona. But having a friend to talk to would be so nice."

"We'll make it happen," I promised the little fluff-ball. "So one important question, Joey: where was Ona last night?"

"Right here, of course. I told you, she never leaves the apartment."

"Just like Greta Garbo," said Dooley.

"Not quite. Garbo was often out and about, walking all across New York. She liked peace and quiet, but she wasn't a recluse, like Ona has turned into."

We were silent for a moment, as we looked at the still statuesque figure of Ona gracefully gliding up to us, as if she was on the catwalk. She knelt down, and placed a bowl filled with what looked like balls of meat in front of us.

"That's my favorite food!" Joey cried. "Straight from the best caterer in town!"

"Well, dig in," I said. I know I was going to. All this talk, and especially climbing that fire escape, had given me a serious appetite.

And so the three of us shared this delicious meal.

"What's in this?" asked Dooley when the last meatball had been eaten. "Cause Max and I are vegetarians, you see, so we don't eat meat."

Joey frowned at my friend. "These are meatballs, Dooley."

"Uh-huh. So what's in these meatballs?"

"Why, meat, of course."

Dooley laughed. "Meat doesn't look like that. No, seriously. What's in it?"

I interrupted, "So you're one hundred percent sure Ona didn't leave the apartment last night?"

"One thousand percent. Unfortunately."

"Not even to go for a midnight stroll around the block?"

"Not even for a midnight stroll."

"So who takes you out for a walk?"

"She's hired a dog walker. A very nice lady who loves dogs." She smiled. "In fact it's the only time I get to socialize. Apart from now with you guys, of course."

I had one more obligatory question to ask. "Can you think of anyone who would hurt Michael Madison, Joey?"

"Apart from Ona, you mean?" She thought for a moment. "Not really. He was well-liked, as far as I know. In fact Ona liked him a lot, too. Until he told her to have this operation."

"But why? Wasn't she beautiful enough?"

"I thought she was. But what do I know? I'm just a dog."

"Sometimes beautiful people want to look even more beautiful," said Dooley. "And then they have cosmetic procedures they don't really need. It's sad, really."

"It is sad," said Joey.

We studied Ona, as she sat on a lounge chair on her balcony, reading a book and sporting oversized sunglasses that obscured the upper portion of her famous face. "Maybe a new medical procedure can undo the damage that was done?" I suggested.

"Ona has consulted with the best doctors on the planet. They all agree that there's considerable risk involved if she gets more work done on her face. The important thing right now is to give the skin tissue time to heal. Then maybe after a while she can go in and they can try and fix some of the things that went wrong."

"So there's hope, at least," I said.

"Oh, absolutely," said Joey. "I mean, Ona is the most positive person I know. She doesn't feel she'll look like this forever, or be locked up inside here forever. At some point she hopes she can put this whole ordeal behind her."

"And in the meantime we'll make sure she adopts a friend for you," I said.

The little furry doggie actually teared up at this. "So kind," she murmured. "You guys are so, so kind."

And so we found ourselves in the unlikely position of having to comfort a dog. Then again, I guess it's all par for the course when you're a feline sleuth!

CHAPTER 25

Our quest for the truth continued, and this time our subject was Doris Booth. We met up with the former editor in a cozy tea room, where she had agreed to meet Odelia for a tell-all interview about the lawsuit she had filed against Michael Madison. Though now that the CEO was dead, I wondered if the lawsuit would still go ahead. Hard to sue a dead person, I would have imagined.

Underneath the table, a teacup doggie sat eyeing us with misty eyes. It looked like a tiny ball of fluff, but unlike Joey didn't respond to our presence with hostility but unveiled curiosity.

"Hey, there," I said as we settled in for the duration of the interview.

"Hi," said the doggie, who was of uncertain breed.

Introductions were made, and the dog turned out to answer to the unlikely name Froufrou. She was nice enough, and soon we enjoyed a cozy little chat.

"So Madison is dead, huh?" said Froufrou. "Well, as much as I hate to say it, good riddance, Max."

"But why?" asked Dooley. "I know we only met him briefly, but he seemed like a good person."

"Good person! He gave Doris a copy of *Elements of Style*! Basically telling her she can't write. That's not the kind of thing you do to a person. Totally out of line."

"Can Doris write?" I asked.

"Of course she can! She's the best writer I know."

Which wasn't saying much, of course, since Doris was probably the only writer Froufrou knew. Still, it was admirable to see such loyalty in man's best friend.

"Did Doris kill Michael Madison, you think?" asked Dooley.

Froufrou gave him a look of amusement. "You don't beat around the bush, do you, Dooley?"

"I believe in the direct approach," my friend said. "Humans circle round and round and sniff each other's butts for hours before they get down to brass tacks but not me."

"I think you'll find that's actually dogs," said Froufrou. "Especially the butts part. But to answer your question: no, Doris did not murder Michael Madison. She was getting even with the man, but she wasn't going to stoop as low as that. And besides, now that he's dead, her wrongful dismissal suit is probably going out the window."

"She can still sue Advantage," I suggested.

"And she will. But with Michael gone, they'll claim it was his decision and his decision alone, and they had nothing to do with it."

"So she was home last night—all night?" I asked.

"She was home last night," Froufrou confirmed. "We Netflixed and chilled."

I stared at the doggie "You mean…"

"We watched a Netflix movie and relaxed on the couch."

"Oh, right," I said, much relieved. I didn't think Doris was into any funny business, but one can never be sure, of course. "Netflix and chill. Gotcha."

"We Netflix and chill all the time," said Dooley.

I grimaced. This conversation was getting off track.

"Or at least Odelia and Chase do, and we stick around."

Our humans seemed to have concluded their conversation, and so it was time to leave. But Froufrou had one parting shot to deliver. "Doris is much better off since she left Advantage. Did you know that the day after she quit she was hired by Advantage's big competitor? She writes for *Glam* now, and no one has accused her of not being able to spell yet. So it's all to the good."

All to the good, except for Michael Madison, who was dead.

Then again, one person's misfortune is often another person's fortune.

CHAPTER 26

We caught Wayne Piscina on his break. The former assistant photographer was working for a local catering company now, delivering meals at home. He might even be the one delivering meals to Ona Konpacka. He was dressed in a snazzy orange outfit, hoisting a bulky orange backpack.

Odelia seated herself on the park bench next to the disgraced assistant, and launched into her spiel.

"Look, I don't know what you heard," said Mr. Piscina, "but there was no scandal, and I wasn't fired, okay? I quit. Creative differences. Mike Madison was a tough man to please, and I just couldn't function in the kind of toxic environment he created around himself."

"So you quit and now you're working as a delivery guy?"

"Hey, it's a great job. You're out and about, on your bike, plenty of exercise and fresh air. If there's one thing you should know about me, it's that I'm a people pleaser, and there's nothing more gratifying than delivering a great meal and watching those happy faces when you arrive on their doorstep with their meal."

"So that story about the tweets?"

"Lies—all lies. Never happened."

"I've got some of those tweets here," said Odelia, taking out her phone. "Looks like someone took a bunch of screenshots before you removed your account."

Wayne eyed her nervously, his back stiffly pressed against the bench. Finally he relented. "Okay, so maybe those tweets exist. But like I explained already to anyone who'll listen, I was young and stupid when I fired off those tweets. Young, *drunk* and stupid, I might add. And I apologize unreservedly. Absolutely. But to fire me over some old tweets? Come on. That's just ridiculous. You might as well come after me for stealing Nickie Marshall's Barbie doll in second grade."

"So you admit that you were fired now?"

"Yeah, okay. So I was fired. There. Happy now? You got your quote?"

"It's not about quotes, Wayne. Mike Madison died last night, and rumor has it he didn't jump but was pushed. So at some point the police will be looking at you."

"I know, I know," said Wayne, dragging a hand through a shaggy mane of dark hair. He sat forward. "Look, I didn't kill him, if that's what you're implying. Okay, so he fired me over some stupid old tweets, and I was unhappy with the guy, hoping he'd have more backbone than that. But I'm not going around murdering people, okay? Like I said, I'm a people *pleaser*, not a people killer."

"One doesn't exclude the other," she pointed out.

He barked a humorless laugh. "Nice. Very nice. Anyway, I can prove it wasn't me. When was he killed?"

"Around three o'clock last night."

"Bingo." He had taken out his phone. "At three o'clock I was delivering a meal to..." He tapped his phone. "Ian McCluster. Three-course meal from Delmonica's."

"At three o'clock at night?"

"Sure. You'd be surprised how many people order meals in the middle of the night. Those are the best shifts, by the way. Extra pay and extra tips for the tip jar."

"So if I contact Ian McCluster he'll confirm that you were on his doorstep at three o'clock last night?" When Wayne nodded, she added, "What's the address?"

After he'd given her the address, she closed her notebook, and shook the guy's hand. And then he was off, to deliver another meal to another happy customer.

"What do you think?" I asked after Wayne had mounted his bike and left.

"Ian McCluster lives awfully close to Advantage Publishing headquarters," said Odelia. "In fact according to Google Maps Wayne could have reached there in less than twenty minutes, after delivering that three-course meal from Delmonica's."

"So he's a prime suspect?"

Odelia shrugged. "Too soon to tell, but he's definitely on the list."

Our next port of call was the Mitchell home. Scarlett had told Odelia to go easy on Tom, since he was probably suffering an acute attack of lovesickness. But still, he was a potential suspect, and so he needed to be interviewed by our relentless reporter!

We found the whole family home, all living under the same roof in a modest row house in one of the less agreeable neighborhoods in Hampton Cove. The streets were clean, though, and the house was nice enough once you stepped inside.

Tom's mom Melanie was a voluminous woman with a ready smile and a homey demeanor. She clearly loved her son Tom and his little brother Harry, and also Danny, the cousin, Advantage's mailroom maven.

"So I just wanted to ask you a couple of questions," said Odelia once we were all seated in the living room, which centered around a very large flat-screen television where some football game was silently playing. "You know that Michael Madison died last night?"

Melanie Mitchell nodded fervently. "Danny told us the news. Bad business. Really bad. Do you have any idea when the boys will be able to go back to work?"

"Mrs. Kingsley doesn't work for Advantage, Mom," said Tom.

"I know, but maybe she heard something."

"I have no idea," Odelia confessed.

"They have to find a new boss first," said Danny. "And knowing Advantage that won't take long. Big conglomerates like that have contingency plans for these types of situations."

"Suicide situations, you mean?" asked Melanie.

"Death of a CEO type of situations. CEOs get killed all the time. They break their necks skiing in Vail, or burn to death when their private jet falls from the sky, or they choke to death on a caviar sandwich. Very risky being a CEO."

"I didn't know people ate caviar on a sandwich," said Harry, who was Tom's little brother, and looked about twelve, though in actual fact he was fifteen. He was chewing his nails, and clearly wanted to be elsewhere right now.

"You can eat caviar on anything," said Danny. "Toast, a sandwich, fries…."

This had Harry burst out laughing. "Caviar and fries! No way!"

"Okay, so rumor has it," said Odelia, trying to get the conversation back on track, "that Madison didn't jump, but was actually pushed out of his window."

Silence greeted these words, then Melanie said, "What do you mean?"

"She means he was pushed, Mom," said Tom.

"But what does that mean?"

"It means he was killed," said Danny. "Isn't that what you mean, Mrs. Kingsley?"

Odelia confirmed that this was what she meant, and Melanie gasped, clutching a hand to her throat. "But that means... he was murdered!"

"Yes, Auntie Mel," said Danny. "That's usually what happens when you're pushed out of a window and end up dead."

"But why? And who? And... oh, God, what does this mean!"

"That's what I'm trying to find out," said Odelia, glad to get that part of the conversation out of the way.

"I thought you said he jumped?" said Harry, crossing his arms in front of his chest.

"That's what I was told," said Danny. "But clearly Mrs. Kingsley heard different."

"Was there a witness?" asked Tom. "Someone who saw what happened?"

Dooley and I shared a look, but Odelia answered smoothly, "I don't know. I'm just telling you what I heard. So can you think of anyone who'd hurt Mr. Madison? You, Tom?"

Tom shrugged. "I can think of a lot of people who didn't like Madison. I didn't like him, for instance."

"But Tommy, you didn't kill him!" said his mother.

"Of course I didn't kill him, Mom," said Tom. "But that's not the question. The question is if we can think of anyone who'd harm Madison. And to be honest, I could. Though I wouldn't, of course," he hastened to add.

"You didn't like how he treated Natalie Ferrara, did you?" asked Odelia softly.

Tom nodded and looked away. "I hated him for what he did to her. First getting her pregnant, then breaking up with her and telling her to get an abortion? Who does that?"

"He wasn't a kind man," Danny confirmed.

"Can I go now?" asked Harry, who clearly wasn't interested in this part of the conversation.

"No, you're going to stay put," said Melanie, "and listen." She gave Odelia a look of apology. "Don't mind him. Harry can't wait to get back to his computer." She ruffled her youngest son's hair, who made a face and pulled away. "He's the hacker in the family, aren't you?"

"How many times, Mom? I'm not a hacker," said Harry. "I'm an online investor."

"Of course you are," said Melanie. "Harry wants to become a millionaire," she announced, regarding her son affectionately. "Isn't that right, sweetie?"

"Yeah, whatever," said her son with an eyeroll.

"Okay, so how about you, Danny?" asked Odelia. "Can you think of anyone who'd wanna hurt Madison?"

"Do you want a list?" said Danny. "The guy wasn't exactly Mr. Popular." He gave us a few of the names on his list, but it turned out Odelia already had them on hers, so there wasn't a lot of news to be extracted from this scion of the Mitchell family. "Though personally I'd put my money on Deith," Tom's cousin concluded.

"Madison's wife?"

"Absolutely. You should have seen them yesterday, fighting like cats and dogs in his office, and she didn't care if his entire staff heard them."

"It's always so sad when husband and wife fight," said Melanie. "Sad for the kids, I mean."

"Do you have anything concrete to support these suspicions?" asked Odelia.

"No, just my general knowledge of human nature," said Danny. "The woman is evil, Mrs. Kingsley. And if she found out about her husband's affair with Natalie, there's no telling what she would do to get even." He straightened and held up a finger. "Hell hath no fury like a woman scorned. That's Shakespeare for you."

"Congreve," said his cousin quietly.

"Who?"

"William Congreve," Tom said. "Not William Shakespeare."

"Huh. How about that?"

"Okay, so now for one final question," said Odelia, "but an important one. Where were you guys last night, when all this happened?"

Danny grinned widely. "Seriously? You're asking about our alibis?"

"You're not accusing us of murder, are you?" asked Melanie.

"I'm not accusing you of anything," said Odelia. "It's just a routine question. Just a matter of excluding you from my inquiries."

"You sound like a cop," Harry muttered darkly.

"Well, if you have to know, we were right here," said Melanie. "Sound asleep in our beds, just like we always are at that time of night. Isn't that right, boys?"

Three heads obediently bobbed up and down.

"So no one left the house last night?" asked Odelia.

"Absolutely not," said Melanie. "And I would know if they did. I'm a light sleeper, you see. If one of the boys goes to the bathroom I wake up. My husband Jim always told me to use earplugs. He didn't understand I don't mind waking up. I like to know that if anything happens my boys can count on me.

Jim, rest his soul—he died ten years ago next week and I still miss him every day—he fell off a roof, you know—we sued the construction company, of course, but nothing doing."

"Mom!" said Tom. "Get to the point already!"

"Right. What was I saying?"

"Something about earplugs?" Harry suggested with a wicked grin.

"Earplugs? Now why would I talk about earplugs?"

"You said you'd know if one of your boys left the house last night," Odelia said helpfully.

"Oh, right! Well, I would, wouldn't I? The least little noise and I'm wide awake. But I don't mind. Jim always told me to use earplugs—ah, now I see where I was going with this—well, anyway, he fell off that roof through no fault of his own and I still miss him every day." Her eyes had grown moist, and she now pulled a Kleenex from a box on the coffee table and pressed it to her nose. "And then when my sister and her husband died... Car crash." She nodded emphatically. "They were both dead on impact. We sued the other driver but nothing doing. Anyway..."

"So nobody left the house, because you would have heard if they did, and you don't know who killed Michael Madison," Odelia summed up the state of affairs.

"It's not easy raising three boys on your own," Melanie posited. "But I like to think I did a good job."

"You did a great job, Mom," said Tom, who seemed the most sensible of the trio. He patted his mom on the back, and more tears formed in the woman's eyes. Soon she was sniffling and snuffling, much to the embarrassment of the three young men gathered around her.

"That's what you get from watching those soaps all the time," Danny declared earnestly. "They turn your mind to mush."

"Hey, watch your tongue, young man!" said Melanie, then

seemed to collect herself. "You'll stay for dinner, of course, Mrs. Kingsley," she said.

"Oh, no," said Odelia. "I couldn't."

"Nonsense. Skinny little thing like you? It's obvious you haven't had a decent meal in ages. If you were living under my roof I'd fatten you right up. Put some meat on those bones."

Odelia didn't seem to want fattening up, and after some wrangling, managed to escape the woman's hospitality unscathed and so did we.

We had one more person to talk to, you see, and I had a feeling Deith Madison wasn't the kind of woman who liked to be kept waiting!

CHAPTER 27

We met Madison's wife in the driveway in front of her majestic villa. She was on her way out, and when we arrived, gave Odelia a supercilious look, before declaring, "I'm not a difficult person, Mrs. Kingsley, but I do appreciate punctuality. So I'm afraid we'll have to do this some other time."

"I just need five minutes of your time," Odelia hastened to say.

Deith Madison ostensively checked her watch, then said, "Make it three."

"Witnesses told us that you and your husband had a row yesterday in his office. Would you care to elaborate what that row was about?"

"No, I would not. What happens between husband and wife is nobody's business except theirs. Next."

"Could it have something to do with the fact that your husband's girlfriend Natalie Ferrara is expecting his baby?"

The woman's mask didn't crack, indicating an extreme level of self-control. "I don't know where you get your information, but I can assure you it's all filth and lies. And if you dare to print any of this, I'll sue you and your paper into oblivion. Last question!"

"Where were you last night, Mrs. Madison?"

For the first time emotion flashed across the woman's face. I interpreted it as surprise. She quickly regained her poise. "Not that it's any of your business, but I was home last night."

"Alone?"

"Since my husband was in the habit of working late at the office, it wasn't unusual for me to spend my nights alone. So yes, I was home alone last night. Now if there's nothing further," she said, walking to a waiting yellow Mercedes.

"Rumor has it that your husband didn't kill himself, Mrs. Madison, but that he was pushed. Care to comment?"

This seemed to spark her interest. "Who told you this?"

Odelia shrugged. "A reliable source."

Deith studied Odelia carefully before responding. "Please share your suspicions with the police. I find it hard to believe Michael would have killed himself. He wasn't the type." She got into the Mercedes, and before long we were being sprayed with gravel as she drove off at a respectable rate of speed.

"What do you think?" asked Odelia, as we stared after the disappearing car.

"She seemed truthful enough," I said. "Except for the part about the pregnancy. I'm pretty sure she knew all about that, and that's what that fight was about."

"I agree," said Odelia. "But until we get her into the police station, she'll never admit to that."

"So why don't you make a citizen's arrest?" Dooley suggested as we got back into our own car.

Odelia laughed. "You need to have probable cause to make an arrest, Dooley. A suspicion that someone is lying isn't enough."

"I think she did it," my friend insisted. "She found out about that pregnancy, and got so upset she shoved him out of that window."

"It's possible," Odelia agreed as she started up the car. "But we need more than a hunch to make an arrest. We need evidence, and a solid case against Deith."

"You'll get there," Dooley assured her. "I have every confidence in you, Odelia."

Odelia grinned. "Why, thank you, Dooley. That's very nice to hear."

And since our interview with Deith was cut short, she decided to squeeze in one more person before she called it a day.

That person was Natalie Ferrara, who featured high on our list.

Unfortunately for us we didn't find Natalie home. We did find her brother Luke though, who had reluctantly dragged himself up from the couch to answer the door, and resumed his position the moment we walked in. He was watching the same football game the Mitchells had been watching, only he was surrounded by junk wherever you looked: plates with half-eaten sandwiches, empty plastic wrappers, pizza boxes, cans of beer and soda, an overflowing ashtray on the table, and a pervasive smell of marijuana causing me to cough the moment we entered.

Looked like Natalie's brother wasn't exactly making himself useful!

"Nat's out," he said as he took a sip from a container of beer. "I can give her a message if you want."

"No, that's all right," said Odelia, looking around for a place to sit, but not finding any.

Luke burped. "Want pizza? You'll have to shove it in the microwave if you want it hot, though."

"I'm fine," Odelia assured him. "So you heard about what happened to Michael Madison?"

"Who? Oh, that guy. Yeah, he died, right?"

"He did. Sometime late last night."

"Uh-huh," Luke said, not showing the least bit of interest.

"So where were you guys last night?" asked Odelia casually.

"Here," said Luke.

"You and your sister both?"

"Sure. Where else would we be?"

"You didn't go out?"

"Nope. Had some friends over. Had a little party. Slept."

When nothing more seemed forthcoming, Odelia decided to broach a sensitive subject. "Did Natalie tell you about her affair with Madison?"

"Uh-huh."

"And how did you feel about that?"

He frowned. "What do you mean?"

"When Madison broke it off with your sister."

"Yeah?"

"How did that make you feel?"

"I don't get it," he said, confused.

"Were you upset that your sister's boss got her pregnant and then broke up with her?"

"Why would I be upset about that? It's her life. Nothing to do with me."

"No, I get that, but as her older brother—"

"Younger."

"As her younger brother, you might have been upset with Madison."

"Well, I wasn't, all right? Frankly I didn't care. If she

wanted to have an affair with her boss—incidentally the oldest cliché in the book—that was her business."

"She was clearly upset, though."

He frowned. "Okay, so who are you, exactly? And why the third degree?"

Patiently, Odelia once more explained who she was, causing the kid to groan with annoyance.

"Just get lost, okay? If I'd known you were a reporter I'd never have let you in."

"Who did you think I was?"

"How should I know? Natalie's friend or whatever. But you're clearly not a friend, so you can just get lost." And as we removed ourselves from the apartment, as requested, he yelled after us, "And don't come back!"

Frankly I had no intention of going back to talk to this annoying individual, and neither had Odelia. I felt sorry for Natalie, though, who had to live with this guy.

"Family isn't always everything, is it, Max?" said Dooley as Odelia drove us home.

"No, it's not," I agreed.

"Poor Natalie."

"Yeah, poor Natalie."

Dooley turned to Odelia. "If your investigation reveals Natalie as Michael Madison's killer, maybe you can hold off on having her arrested until she kills her brother, too."

Odelia laughed at this. "Thanks for the tip, Dooley. But I don't think that's entirely legal."

"No, but it's the right thing to do," my friend returned.

Maybe he had a point. With family like that, who needs enemies?

CHAPTER 28

Before going home, though, Odelia decided to make a detour by the police precinct, to discuss the case with her husband and uncle. And so we found ourselves in Uncle Alec's office for the second time in one day.

And as Odelia gave the two cops an extensive report of her findings, it soon became clear that she'd been liaising with Chase all the while, and the latter hadn't been idle either. He'd been checking the alibis of the suspects Odelia had interviewed, and the result was thus: Gary Rapp had indeed spent the night drinking at a bar with some lovely ladies, but had left at two, which would have given him plenty of time to slip back to the office and kill his former boss.

Wayne Piscina hadn't lied when he said he delivered a meal to a late client, and that same late client had confirmed his story as had Piscina's new boss. His route had taken him pretty close to Advantage headquarters, though, so who was to say he hadn't paid a visit to his old boss, gotten into an argument and shoved him out of his window? It would also explain the lack of badge activity, if Madison had personally buzzed his late-night visitor in and taken him up to his office.

Though the same went for Gary Rapp, of course.

"Okay, so as far as the others are concerned," said Odelia, checking her notes, "Deith Madison was home alone—which we need to check. Natalie Ferrara was home with her brother—at least according to the brother. I haven't managed to get a hold of her. Tom Mitchell was home with his family." She looked up with a smile of amusement. "His mom went to great lengths to explain how she's a light sleeper and would have heard if Tom left the house at any point last night."

"And the same applies to Danny, I suppose," said Chase.

"Is he a suspect?" asked Uncle Alec.

"Not really," said Odelia. "Unless he felt so bad for his cousin that he would go out and murder his boss. Which seems unlikely."

"Agreed," said the Chief.

"Okay, so we have Doris Booth, whose dog Froufrou confirms she was home all night."

"Froufrou," the Chief murmured, shaking his head. "If anyone heard us, they'd think we're crazy."

"Another pet called Joey, a miniature Brussels Griffon, confirmed that Ona Konpacka didn't leave her apartment," she continued, ignoring her uncle's groans of dismay. She flipped through her notes. "Um… So we need to talk to Deith again, and confirm her alibi, maybe by talking to one of her servants, which I assume she has—she denied knowing about the pregnancy, but I'm pretty sure she was lying. And then there's Howard White."

"*The* Howard White?" asked Chase, sitting up a little straighter.

"I'm surprised you've heard of Howard White," said Odelia, amused.

"I'm a New Yorker born and bred, babe. Of course I've heard of Howard White. The guy is a national treasure."

"He was seen rowing with Michael Madison in the latter's office a couple of days ago. Something about a bad review of the man's latest collection. Madison personally wrote that review, and Mr. White was not amused, to say the least."

"So we'll have to go and talk to the guy," said Chase.

"Do it first thing tomorrow," the Chief suggested. "The sooner we can put this case to rest, the better. I'm already starting to get calls from people wanting to know why my niece is going round claiming Madison's death wasn't suicide."

Odelia grimaced. "I'm sorry, Uncle Alec. I know you told me not to mention it."

"That's fine. We need to get people talking, and if that's the way to do it, so be it." He slapped his desk. "So. Suspects, people?"

Odelia shared a look with her husband. "For my money I'd say Gary Rapp, Deith Madison, or Wayne Piscina."

"Agreed," said Chase. "And let's add Howard White as a possible suspect, pending our interview with the guy. And let's not rule out Natalie Ferrara, if her brother is really as flaky as you say he is."

"He is."

"And we'll scratch Doris Booth, Ona Konpacka and the Mitchells. Okay?"

The trio were in agreement, and so the meeting was adjourned.

"Too bad these other suspects don't have pets," said Dooley. "They could have confirmed their alibis, too. Which just goes to show it's always a good idea to have a pet."

"I like your thinking, Dooley," I said.

"So what's going on with my sister?" asked Uncle Alec. "Is she still upset with Tex about those letters?"

"I think Marge is ready to forgive and forget," said Chase. "After all, it wasn't entirely his fault. In fact it may have been me who put out that box."

"You did this?" asked Odelia.

"It's possible. Though if I did, I had no idea how important the box was."

"They'll work it out," said Odelia. "They always do."

"If there's one thing I know, it's that your dad didn't do it on purpose," said Uncle Alec.

"Just a case of Tex being Tex," said Chase with a grin.

※

Marge, who'd had a long day at the library, arrived home feeling tired and in a bad mood. More people had showed up wanting to know about those letters. Turns out several people had taken pictures of the letters they had found in their mailboxes and had started sharing them on social media. And now all of a sudden it felt as if the whole world was talking about them!

She entered the house through the front door, and was surprised to find the hallway smelling of flowers. And not just any flowers, but pink roses—her favorite! A big bouquet was on the hallway sideboard, and she felt her mood perk up immediately as she took a deep sniff of the blessed blooms.

She dropped her keys in the tray and walked into the living room. She halted in the doorway when she caught sight of several more vases filled with pink and orange roses greeting her from all around the room. There was dozens of them, and the smell was simply amazing!

"Oh, Tex," she murmured, for there was no doubt in her mind that this was her husband's doing, to apologize for the letter business.

She took a peek into the kitchen, to see if Tex was

around, and what she found were even more roses—on the table, on the kitchen island—everywhere!

The door opened, and her ma walked in, a big smile on her face. "Hey, honey," she said. "Nice surprise?"

"The best," she said, perking all up.

"He's in the backyard," said Ma.

She nodded and took a sniff from a nearby bouquet, plucked a single rose from the bunch, then walked out.

Tex was seated on the porch swing, looking moody. When he became aware of her, his frown turned into a smile, though. A hopeful smile. "Did you see…"

She nodded.

"What do you…"

"I like."

He blinked a few times, and she saw he had teared up. She smiled and put her hand on his cheek, which he kissed tenderly. There was not an ounce of malice in this man. Not a single drop. He was her absentminded professor, and she loved him dearly. And just like that, she realized her anger had dissipated and was gone.

She sat down next to him and took his hand. She then put her head on his shoulder. And so they sat like that for a couple of minutes, in grateful silence.

"I'm sorry," he said. "I should have been more careful with your letters."

"Your letters, you mean."

"The moment I sent them to you, they became yours."

"I love those letters," she said, as she kissed his cheek.

"I love you," he said quietly.

"And I love you," she returned.

And when her mother took a peek through the kitchen window a few moments later, and saw her daughter and son-in-law seated together on the swing, the old lady smiled, pumped the air with her fist, and whispered, "Yes!"

CHAPTER 29

Howard White, the celebrated designer, occupied two floors of an impressive brownstone in the heart of Greenwich Village. The big man was expecting us, and his assistant Sebastian was already supplying our humans with coffee in small porcelain cups the moment we walked in.

"Oh, this is just gorgeous," Odelia exclaimed when she took in the expansive loft space, which was uninhibited by inner walls or even columns, and afforded a stunning view of the local park. Plenty of light streamed in, and everywhere we looked we could see framed designs by the master's hand adorning the walls.

"We like it here," Sebastian announced modestly, indicating that perhaps he wasn't merely Mr. White's assistant but something more. "Of course we got it when prices were still affordable in this part of town. If we were to sell, we'd probably fetch an inordinate sum, considering how much prices have gone up. But we've lived here for so long now we'd never leave. Isn't that so, chouchou?"

Chouchou turned out to be the artist himself, who now

emerged from upstairs, where presumably his living quarters were located. Howard White was a tall man, with distinguished white hair and a long, impassive, tan face. I would have guessed he was in his early sixties, and I don't think I would have been far off.

"Greetings, Mrs. Kingsley—Mr. Kingsley," he said in clipped tones as he shook hands with our humans, then held out those same hands for Sebastian to squirt some clear liquid from a bottle, then efficiently wipe them with disinfectant wipes. The whole process passed so quickly that it was obvious this was a common thing in the White household. "How may I be of assistance?" he asked.

Sebastian gestured to a brown leather sofa, which looked more like a work of art than an actual comfy couch, and our humans carefully took a seat, with Mr. White and Sebastian taking up position on the opposing sofa.

The artist then seemed to notice myself and Dooley for the first time, for he made a face and expressed his abhorrence by saying, "Cats! Nobody told me there would be cats!"

And here I thought all humans loved cats.

"They're perfectly groomed specimens," Sebastian assured the big man. "I've checked them myself and they're clean—no sign of lice or parasites of any kind." He handed Mr. White a document, which I recognized as the form Odelia had had to fill out before she could be allowed to meet with the famous designer.

The designer waved it away. "Fine, fine," he said impatiently. He rested his perfectly manicured hands in his lap and sat back with a serene expression on his face. "Please begin," he said, and awaited further proceedings.

"We're investigating the death of Michael Madison," said Chase. "A man you're probably familiar with."

"Of course," said the designer, inclining his head. "Michael and I go way back."

"Which is why it came as something of a shock to us," said Odelia, "that Michael wrote critically about your latest collection. An article that probably didn't go down well with you, sir?"

"That's correct," said the designer. "When I read the article, I was shocked. *Glimmer* has been a mainstay in my career going back forty years, and I've always had an excellent working relationship with its subsequent editors."

"Before Michael Madison became CEO of the entire Advantage group, he worked as editor-in-chief for *Glimmer*," Sebastian explained.

"And in that capacity he never had a bad word to say about my work," said Howard with a frown.

"And then all of a sudden he was promoted CEO of the group, and *Glimmer's* attitude toward our work took a violent turn," said Sebastian. "Isn't that true, chouchou?"

"Almost as if Michael felt he had something to prove now that he was in charge. It's very unusual, you see, that a CEO would get involved in the day-to-day business of producing copy for his flagship magazine."

"He didn't even have the guts to write the piece under his own name," Sebastian scoffed. "He used a pseudonym. At first we thought another editor had written it."

"Gary Rapp."

"Yes. But it was Michael, all right. Writing this dreadful hatchet piece."

"So I called him," said Howard. "I wanted to know what he thought he was doing. First he denied having written the piece. Claimed he hadn't even read it, and was going to 'investigate,' before getting back to me."

"He never got back to us," said Sebastian.

"And so I paid him a visit in his lair."

"He wasn't happy."

"I wasn't happy. And I gave it to him with both barrels."

"Do you know what his excuse was?" asked Sebastian, quirking a finely penciled eyebrow. "He said *Glimmer* had to move with the times. That they couldn't cater to dinosaurs forever, and had to focus on new, more *exciting* designers. And since no one dared to write the truth, he figured he'd do it himself."

"I'm not a dinosaur," said Howard White, lifting his chin.

"Of course not, chouchou," Sebastian assured him. "If anyone is a dinosaur in this story, it's Michael Madison."

"Was," said Chase.

"Yes, was," said Sebastian, demurely casting down his eyes.

"I like to think I've always kept my finger on the pulse of the fashion industry," said Howard. "Tried hard not to get stuck in the past. But obviously Michael thought differently, and decided to fire a shot across the bow. Let me know that I was now officially a has-been. A talentless hack. An old fossil." He carefully studied his fingers. "Look who's the has-been now," he said softly.

"I guess Michael simply couldn't take the pressure," said Sebastian, and there was a touch of satisfaction in his tone. "It's one thing to be an editor, but something else to be in charge of the entire company. Especially in an industry in decline. Just like in the rest of the publishing industry, circulation of Advantage Publishing's magazines has been dropping precipitously. It's not inconceivable that at some point, if they don't manage to turn things around, they'll be extinct."

"Let's hope it won't come to that," said Howard. "It would be a bad thing for the fashion industry if magazines like *Glimmer* and *Glitter* go out of business."

"The thing is," said Chase now, as he leaned forward, "that it's entirely possible that Michael Madison didn't kill himself." He let his statement hang in the air for a moment, before dropping his bombshell. "But that he was, in fact, murdered."

Howard's cool demeanor cracked a little. "Murdered!" he exclaimed.

"Well, what do you know?" said Sebastian, looking oddly pleased.

"But I thought he jumped? Left a suicide note?" said Howard.

"We have reason to believe that he may have been pushed. And that whoever killed him faked that suicide note."

"But…" Howard turned to his assistant/partner. "Did you know about this?"

"Absolutely not, chouchou," Sebastian assured the older man. "I had no idea."

Howard turned a pair of keen eyes on Chase. "So that's why you're here. To ask me if I'm the one who killed Michael Madison." He smirked a little. "So are you going to arrest me? Are you here to slap a pair of handcuffs on my wrists?"

"Oh, dear," said Sebastian, who was thoroughly enjoying the drama.

"We're not here to make an arrest today," Chase assured the designer. "We're simply talking to all the people that knew Michael Madison."

"Especially the ones with a reason to kill him?" asked Howard.

"Well…" said Chase. "You did have a public spat."

"More than a spat," said Howard. "I told him that if he ever talked to me like that again, or wrote an article like that about me or my work, I'd sue him for defamation of character and slander. And I told him that if he wanted to make an enemy out of me, he'd better think long and hard first, because I could make life difficult for him, the same way he was trying to make life difficult for me."

"How were you going to make life difficult for Michael?" asked Odelia.

Howard shared a cautious look with Sebastian. They were on tricky ground now, and both seemed to realize it. "*Glimmer* always got the best seats in the house at any of my fashion shows," Howard explained. "They got invites to pre-shows, exclusive previews, behind-the-scenes interviews, access to me and my team, the whole shebang. And since we all know that exclusivity and access sells copies, this was a good deal for both of us. If Michael was going to continue this hostile attitude of his, all of that would be a thing of the past. *Glimmer* would get the same treatment as the rest of the written press. Nothing more, nothing less."

"We were also thinking about denying *Glimmer* access to our models, photographers, designers," said Sebastian. "A strict omertà across the board."

"If Michael really thought I was an old has-been, that wouldn't have mattered to him or *Glimmer*," said Howard. "But if not…" He gave us a meaningful look.

"All of that would come on top of the legal action we threatened to take," said Sebastian. "He immediately backed off when we hit him with that double whammy." He looked defiant now. "Said he didn't mean it like that, and how valuable *Glimmer's* longstanding relationship with Howard White was to him."

"I didn't have to kill the man, detective," said Howard. "I already had him licked!" He had the air of an old lion who still has a few tricks up his sleeve.

"We had him cornered," said Sebastian. "Absolutely cornered!"

Howard leaned forward. "So who killed him, you think?"

"That's what we're trying to find out," said Odelia.

"Which is why we have to ask you where you were two nights ago," Chase said. "You and your assistant both."

Howard and Sebastian shared a look of amusement, and before long they were both laughing heartily, as if Chase had told the funniest joke. "I'm not Howard's assistant," said Sebastian finally. The two men held hands. "I'm his husband."

"Well, not officially," said Howard. "I don't believe in marriage. But yes, Sebastian and I have been together for, oh, going on thirty years now?"

"Thirty-two next month," said Sebastian decidedly. "Which reminds me, what do you want for our anniversary, chouchou?"

"You know me. Nothing special," said the designer.

Sebastian turned to us. "That's what he always says. But then when I don't organize the most fabulous party, he gets all moody and sad, the big chouchou."

"I'm sure Mr. and Mrs. Kingsley aren't interested in all that," said Howard.

"Okay, so where were we when Michael was killed?" said Sebastian, lightly slapping his thighs. He glanced over to Howard. "Did we dine out? I can't remember."

"Two nights ago," said Howard, fingering his smoothly shaved chin.

"Ooh, that's right! Two nights ago we watched that French movie. The funny one with Christian Clavier and Chantal Lauby." He turned to us. "We never laughed so hard in our lives. Isn't that right, chouchou?"

"It was very funny," Howard admitted with a smile.

"Hilarious," said Sebastian with satisfaction.

Both men proceeded to beam at us, like two choir boys who've discovered the stock of sacramental wine and have managed to drink it all without being caught.

CHAPTER 30

"I don't understand why we had to travel all the way to New York," Dooley lamented once we were back in the car and on our way to Hampton Cove.

"Because Odelia didn't know if Howard White had pets," I explained.

"I don't get it," Dooley said.

"If Howard had pets, we would have been able to talk to them, and ascertain whether Howard's alibi was valid or not. But now that it turns out that he didn't have pets, you're correct in that our presence wasn't required."

"I don't like traveling by car," Dooley said as he hunkered down in the backseat.

"I don't like it either, buddy," I said.

In fact cats don't like to travel anywhere. Not by car, not by plane, not by any mode of transportation. We basically like to stay home and not move around in these horrible man-made machines. I mean, if God had wanted us to fly, He would have given us wings, and if He wanted us to travel in cars, He would have given us turn signals.

"So what do you think?" asked Odelia as she put the finishing touches to her notes. "On a scale of one to ten, how would you rate Howard as a suspect?"

"I'm not sure," said Chase, hedging his bets as usual. As a detective, he liked to play his cards close to his chest. "I mean, do I think it's likely that he killed Madison? No, I don't. Do I think it's impossible? I don't think so either."

"So what you're actually saying is that you don't think he did it, and yet you think he did."

"I'm just saying I don't know."

"Yeah, that's what I thought."

She frowned before her, then turned to us. "What do you think, Max? On a scale of one to ten, how likely is it that Howard White killed Madison?"

"I don't know," I admitted.

"God," said Odelia. "Nobody knows anything."

"What do you think?" asked Chase as he navigated the Long Island Expressway. "On a scale of one to ten."

"I don't know!" Odelia cried, throwing up her hands, and in the process dislodging her tablet from her lap, and sending it flying into the footwell. "So many suspects, and not a single clue to go on! It's so frustrating!"

"I know," said Chase. "But at least we have suspects. Imagine having a victim but not a single suspect."

"We don't just have one suspect. We have an abundance of suspects," Odelia grumbled. "We're drowning in suspects!"

"Odelia seems stressed," Dooley commented.

"It's not easy to investigate a murder case that isn't officially a murder case, with more suspects than clues, and where every suspect seems to have a good reason to murder the victim," I said.

"This murder case isn't officially a murder case?"

"Oh, no. It's only official if there's a witness, or a strong suspicion that foul play is involved. But the only witness we have is a badger."

"That badger is a strong witness, Max."

"I know. But not in a court of law. And that's what counts."

"Complicated," said Dooley. "It's all very complicated, Max."

"So what do you think, Dooley? On a scale of one to ten?"

"Zero for traveling by car," said Dooley. "And ten for getting home safe and sound."

Now those were numbers I could live with.

"So have your mom and dad reconciled?" asked Chase.

Odelia smiled. "Dad got Mom pink roses. A lot of pink roses. She couldn't stay angry with him after that. And to think those roses were Gran's idea."

"That was very nice of her."

"Gran is often on Dad's case, but actually she's very fond of him."

"Your dad is a great guy, and we're all very fond of him."

Odelia put down her tablet, and for the next half hour, the case was temporarily forgotten, as they discussed family matters instead of murder.

And in spite of the harrowing circumstances, Dooley and I took a long nap.

Once again, Advantage Publishing was open for business. Gran and Scarlett had been invited back, as had the rest of the company's staff, and of course Gran and Scarlett's emotional support animals couldn't be excluded from the roster.

And so Dooley and I were on Gran's desk, taking in the

exciting world of commerce from our vantage point, while Gran and her friend worked like beavers to further the interests of Dear Gabi. They still hadn't given up on their matchmaking efforts, and had come up with a new plan of campaign. Gran would work on Natalie, while Scarlett would focus her attentions on Natalie's prospective beau Tom.

Michael Madison's office had been completely remodeled—perhaps the fastest remodel in history—with all remnants of the murdered CEO's reign removed. The new CEO hadn't yet taken up their position at the helm, but rumor had it that negotiations had entered the final stage. And so the office was abuzz with wild speculation and gossip about who could possibly become their new boss—always an important aspect of office life!

Scarlett had sashayed up to Tom, and took a seat next to the embattled young man. He looked just as miserable as ever—perhaps it was his signature look?

Scarlett must have thought the key to making him more palatable to Natalie was to do something about his general appearance, for she opened proceedings by saying, "Girls don't like it when a guy looks like a slob, Tom."

"Are you saying I look like a slob?" asked the lovesick editor, glancing down at his costume. He was wearing his usual faded jeans, a T-shirt that announced that he favored Team Chewbacca, whatever Team Chewbacca was, and his hair telegraphed that it hadn't been touched since he stepped out of bed that morning: one side was up, the other was down. Not exactly the hot stud most girls favor!

"You need a haircut, stat," said Scarlett, subjecting him to an uber-critical look. "You need a change of clothes—a change of style, in fact. And you need to stop looking like the end of the world is near and it's happening on your block."

"I haven't been feeling so well," he said. "And I guess it shows."

"It shows. Badly. So let me take you to my favorite hairstylist. And my favorite boutique. And let me give you a couple of books to read that will buck up your self-confidence and put a pep in your step."

"I don't want a pep in my step," he said morosely. "I just want Natalie to talk to me without mentioning the name 'Michael Madison' every second sentence."

"That's going to take time," said Scarlett. "The love of her life just died, so you can't expect her to just get up one morning and fall madly in love with you. But in due course, I think she might be induced to move you out of the friend zone."

"I'm not even in the friend zone right now," said the kid. "I'm in the 'you don't exist' zone. The zone where a meteor just struck and wiped out all sign of life."

See what I mean? Depressed is the best word for it. And a depressed individual has never been able to interest another individual to see him as a love interest. Especially when that other individual is also depressed because the love of her life, as Scarlett so rightly indicated, has just been shoved out of a window.

"If Tom murdered Michael," said Dooley, "because he was hoping that with him out of the picture Natalie would turn to him looking for a shoulder to cry on, he's going to be very disappointed."

"Yeah, whatever shoulder she wants to cry on, it's not Tom's," I agreed.

We glanced in the direction of Natalie, and saw that she was getting up from her desk, and as she passed Gran's desk, the latter also got up, gave us two thumbs up, and followed the personal assistant to the office canteen.

And since Dooley and I were now heavily invested in this

budding office romance, we jumped down from Tom's desk, where we'd eagerly followed Scarlett's attempts to make Tom more suitable as a suitor, and hurried in Gran's wake.

"It's just like a soap, Max," said Dooley. "You just can't wait to see what's going to happen next!"

CHAPTER 31

*I*f Tom looked terrible, Natalie looked even worse. Clearly she hadn't digested the death of her former lover well.

"How are you holding up?" asked Gran solicitously.

"It's Luke," said Natalie as she nursed a cup of coffee. "He invited his friends over for a party again last night, so I didn't sleep a wink."

"Again! But you have to kick him out!" said Gran, aghast.

"I can't. He's got nowhere else to stay," she said miserably.

"Oh, you poor thing," said Gran. Natalie leaned against the sink, and Gran joined her, the two women standing companionably side by side. "It's not been your week, has it, sweetie?"

"You can say that again. Not only do I have to cook, but he won't even wash the dishes, or clean up his mess. And you don't want to know what my apartment looks like. Like a hurricane passed through it. I told him to get it sorted by the time I get home from work, but I can tell you now already that won't happen."

"You have to be stricter with your brother. You can't just let him walk all over you like this."

"Frankly, Vesta, I don't have the strength right now. After what happened with Michael, and then him dying, and the baby, I just feel…" Her voice broke, and as she stared into her cup of coffee, big tears rolled down her cheeks.

"This is just too much," suddenly a voice growled from the door.

When we looked up, we saw that Tom was standing there. He had probably heard the entire conversation, and I could see that he was seeing red.

"Tom," said Natalie, surprised to find her co-worker balling his hands into fists, his face working, and his eyes shooting sheets of flame to no one in particular. The kind, slightly nerdy young man had suddenly turned livid.

"This ends now," Tom announced, and suddenly stomped out.

"What's going on?" asked Gran. "Where is he going?"

"I don't know," said Natalie, a look of concern on her face.

Tom was a fast worker, for not even ten minutes had passed before Natalie got a call from her brother. By then we were all back at our desks—except Tom, who had disappeared.

Natalie came hurrying up to us, her phone pressed to her chest. "It's Luke," she said. "He says some maniac just walked in, and he's threatening to kill him!"

"Uh-oh," said Gran. "That's not good."

It was quite the understatement, and since Natalie seemed in a right state, we decided to accompany the young PA to her home, where her brother was apparently in danger of some grievous bodily harm!

Natalie wasn't in a condition to drive, and so Gran did the honors, setting a world record for traversing from one side of town to the other. When we finally screeched to a halt in front of Natalie's apartment complex, I think we were all a little white around the nostrils.

We staggered from the vehicle, and Natalie hurried up to the front door. But even before we got there, loud voices greeted us from the fifth-floor window.

And as Natalie gasped in shock, suddenly Tom appeared. He had grabbed her brother by the neck and was trying to shove him out the window!

"Tom, don't!" Natalie screamed as Luke held on for dear life.

"Nat, help!" Luke cried. "This maniac wants to kill me!"

"I will kill you," said Tom, "if you don't clear out of your sister's apartment right now. But not before you clean up your mess, and promise never to return!"

"I promise, I promise!" Luke yelled. "But don't kill me, please!"

But Tom wasn't so easily convinced. "If you don't do as I say, I'm coming back, and I will shove you out of this window, and watch your no-good brain splatter on that pavement below. Is that understood, you pathetic waste of skin!"

"Yes, yes! I promise!"

"Good," said Tom, and yanked the kid back inside.

"He's not so meek now," said Dooley.

"No, more like an avenging angel," I said.

"Oh, God," said Natalie, as she hurried to the door.

And as we arrived on the fifth floor, where the drama was unfolding, we were greeted by an apocalyptic scene: the apartment, which hadn't looked all that clean and welcoming before, had been completely trashed! And I had the impression it wasn't Tom who was responsible for the mess.

"He didn't clean up," was the first thing Natalie said when she witnessed the devastation. "I told him to clean up. He promised to clean up. He didn't clean up."

"All the more reason to kick him out," said Gran.

Tom seemed to agree wholeheartedly, for he now greeted us in the hallway, dragging a terrified-looking Luke by the scruff of the neck. "Your brother has something to tell you, Natalie," he announced.

"I'm leaving, Nat," said Luke. "I'm leaving and I'm not coming back."

"But…" Tom prompted.

"But first I'm going to clean up my mess."

"And…"

"And I want to thank you for shopping for me, cooking for me, doing my laundry, and cleaning up after me. But I promise that you won't have to do that anymore."

"Because…"

"Because I'm going to be staying with a friend from now on."

"And…"

"And I want to apologize to you for the trouble I caused."

"And…"

"And I'm going to pay you for all the damages, the food—everything!"

"Good," Tom grunted. "And now get started," he said, and released the young wastrel. Luke produced a sort of yelp of fear, and scuttled into the living room, where he immediately started picking up his trash.

Natalie, who'd watched the scene with slack jaw, now turned eyes filled with gratitude and admiration to Tom, like the rest of us surprised by this sudden transformation the young man had gone through.

"Look, I can't stand this anymore," Tom announced now. "I've never told you this before, Natalie, but I love you. In fact I've loved you from the day you came into my life. The day I started working at Advantage. I've been too chicken to tell you, and to ask you out—until recently. I understand that you're still mourning for Michael. But honestly, I hated the way he treated you. And I hated that he dumped you when you told him you were expecting his baby. The man was a louse. And he didn't deserve you. Just like I don't deserve you. But if I didn't tell you this, I wouldn't be able to live with myself. So…" He shrugged. "I guess now I did."

Natalie nodded quietly. "I knew you liked me, Tom. I've known for a long time. And I think you're a great guy."

Tom's eyes lit up. "So… if I asked you out again sometime. I mean, not now, obviously. But later—once you're feeling better. Do you think… I mean do you…"

"I'm pregnant, Tom. I'm having Michael's baby. I've thought about this a lot, but I'm not going to have the abortion. So this might not be such a good idea."

"I don't mind," said Tom.

"You don't?"

"I don't."

"You don't mind that I'm having another man's baby?"

"Absolutely not. I love you, Natalie. I want to take care of you. You and your baby."

"Oh," said Natalie, and brought a distraught hand to her face. Her eyes were welling up again. And this was the moment Scarlett gave Tom a prod in the ribs, causing that young man to jump forward. He collided with Natalie, and nature did the rest. His arms folded around the young woman, she pressed her face into his chest, and as we watched on, there was hugging, and weeping, and sweet words being exchanged.

"Let's give these two some privacy," said Gran finally, her voice suspiciously husky, and so that's what we did: we all retreated into the living room, where we watched Luke Ferrara go through that room like a human hurricane, picking up litter, collecting broken bottles and crushed beer cans, and generally working harder than he had ever worked before in his life to clean up the mess he and his friends had made. All to avoid being chucked out a fifth-floor window.

Which reminded me. Who else had been chucked out of a window recently?

Exactly.

I could tell that Gran and Scarlett had the same idea I had, for Gran said, "Looks like we've got our killer, hon."

"Too bad," said Scarlett. "Just when young love was in the cards."

"Let's give them a moment before we call the police," Gran suggested.

And so it was decided: Tom might be a killer, but he was also a man in love. And so he might be excused for going around chucking the men who hurt the woman he loved out of windows. Nobody's perfect, after all.

CHAPTER 32

Marge had been busy scanning the books people had returned when Gary Rapp walked in. The man looked as if he'd walked straight out of a romance novel: dove-gray suit, stylishly coiffed, with a killer smile on that confident face.

"I'm not taking no for an answer this time, Marge Poole," he announced as he walked up to her counter. "I've got a great little restaurant picked out for a cozy dinner for two, and I would like very much if you said yes."

"Oh, Gary," said Marge. "I'm flattered, but you know I'm a married woman."

"But not a happily married woman, if my information is correct."

She wavered, but only for a moment. "I am very happy with my husband."

"If I were your husband, I wouldn't casually dump your love letters into the trash," he said, quirking an eyebrow. "Instead I'd remind you every day of my love for you."

"That's very sweet of you, Gary, but—"

"Just say yes, Marge. You know you want to."

She laughed. "You're very persistent, aren't you?"

"I'm a man who knows what he wants. And right now I want you."

"Oh, Gary," she said with a smile. Gary had taken her hand, and was fingering it intently.

"What's going on here?" suddenly a voice boomed behind them. They both jumped at the sound. And when Marge turned, she saw that Tex was standing there, eyeing them with a face that spelled storm. In his hand he was holding a bouquet of pink roses.

"Tex," she said, startled by this unexpected development.

"Marge," said Tex, as he freely ground his teeth, taking in the scene.

Marge tried to extricate her hand from Gary's, but the latter hung onto it, like a trophy. "I think an apology is in order, Poole," said Gary, a steely note in his voice.

"You're absolutely right, Rapp," said Tex. "So you better start apologizing."

"You're the one who owes an apology to your wife. For dumping her letters in the trash, and allowing them to be distributed around the neighborhood, causing her a lot of aggravation and humiliation."

"I already said I'm sorry," said Tex.

"If you really loved your wife, Poole, you wouldn't be so negligent."

Tex's face was working, and Marge, who finally managed to retrieve her hand from Gary's grasp, said, "I know you're sorry, honey. And I forgive you."

"You're being too kind, Marge," said Gary. "Though knowing what a wonderful, kind-hearted woman you are, I shouldn't be surprised. But let me tell you that this man doesn't deserve your forgiveness." He suddenly got down on one knee. "Marge, let me prove to you I'm a better man than your husband will ever be."

"Gary, please…"

"If you wrote me a letter, I would treasure it, not dump it in the trash."

Marge saw Tex wince at these words.

"Just let me prove it to you. Let me take you out to dinner."

She smiled. "Gary, you've been very kind, and very persistent, but I love my husband. Even after twenty-five years, I still love him. Oh, I know he's absentminded sometimes, and does stupid things. But that's all right."

"But he's a moron!"

"I know," she said, darting a smile at her husband. "But he's my moron."

Gary's expression of devotion had melted away, replaced by a scornful look. He abruptly got up and dusted off his nice pair of pants. "Women," he spat. "You're all the same, aren't you? Playing fast and loose with people's affections."

"You better take that back, buddy," said Tex now.

"I'm not taking anything back," said Gary. "Your wife is just like all the other women who pretended to like what I said, and then turned around and filed a complaint against me. Sexual harassment, my foot. You're all a bunch of airheads!"

There was a sort of whirl and a whizzing sound, and the next moment, Gary Rapp stood touching his cheek in surprise. Those nice flowers Tex had been holding now lay on the floor, and red dots appeared on the editor's cheek where the thorns had punctured his skin. "Mano a mano," Tex said, holding up his fists in a pugilistic stance. "You and me, and may the best man win!"

But Gary gave the doctor one scathing look, then turned and left the library.

"Come back here!" Tex cried. "You coward!"

But Gary clearly had no intention to come back and fight

the good doctor. Instead, he slammed the door on his way out.

"That's disappointing," said Tex, who looked thoroughly surprised.

"Oh, Tex," said Marge, as she eyed her husband with gleaming eyes. "That's probably the most romantic thing I've ever seen in my life."

"He said some really bad things about you, honey," said Tex.

"Come here," she said when she saw that his hand was bleeding. And as she kissed the spot, he wrapped her into his arms, and when Margaret Samson emerged from between the racks of books, clutching a tome called 'Dirty Talk,' she found a middle-aged couple fervently kissing, as if they just met for the first time.

The old lady smiled and sighed a happy little sigh.

Sometimes romance happened in real life, too.

CHAPTER 33

*O*delia was walking from her office to the precinct when a gray Mercedes parked next to her and a woman stepped out of the vehicle. She almost bumped into her, and a look of recognition passed over the other person's face.

"Odelia Kingsley, isn't it?" asked Deith Madison.

"Oh, hi, Mrs. Madison," said Odelia. "I've been trying to get a hold of you."

"I know. And I've been trying to stave you off," said the woman with a vague smile. "I should have known that reporters are worse than pit bulls once they've picked up the scent of their prey." She sighed resignedly. "So just ask what you want to ask, and I'll try and answer you as truthfully as possible. How about that?"

"That's all I want," said Odelia, who was feeling inordinately pleased that Deith Madison had compared her to a pit bull. "Last time we spoke you denied that your husband was having an affair with his personal assistant. You called it filth and lies and threatened to sue my newspaper if we dared to print the story."

Deith studied Odelia for a moment, then finally relented. "Michael and I enjoyed a marriage of convenience. He had his affairs and I had mine. And in the meantime we had an understanding that we would never get divorced. It was an arrangement that was mutually beneficial. It provided Michael with the benefit of a vast fortune that I inherited from my side of the family, and it provided me with the connections that he made through the work that he did. So yes, it doesn't surprise me that he was having an affair with his personal assistant."

"Who is now pregnant with his baby."

Deith's expression darkened. "Michael was usually very careful about these things. So when he told me Natalie was pregnant, I have to admit I was upset. We had an arrangement, but that didn't include having kids with other women."

"Which gave you a solid motive for his murder," Odelia pointed out.

Deith threw back her head and laughed. "Oh, honey, if Mike knocking up some girl gave me a motive to murder him, I would have done it a long time ago. This wasn't the first time this happened. And even though I was furious, I wasn't going to kill him over it. So please spare me the amateur detective stuff."

"Were you really home the night your husband was killed, Mrs. Madison?"

"I was," she said. "Michael and I lived separate lives. I lived in my part of the house, and he lived in his. We still spent plenty of time together, but it was an arrangement that suited us both very well." She gave Odelia a look of amusement, then took out her phone and showed her a phone number.

"What's this?" asked Odelia.

"My alibi," said Deith. "It's my boyfriend's number. Call him and he'll confirm that he was with me all night that night. I didn't want to go through the bother of dragging him into this mess, but someone told me you're the chief of police's niece, and that your husband is the detective investigating my husband's death. So before you haul me away, accusing me of all kinds of stuff, please call Alain."

"Alain?" said Odelia, dutifully entering the number into her phone.

"Alain Maury," said Deith. "He won't mind answering your questions. And now if there's nothing else, I would like to talk to my lawyer." When Odelia made to speak, she held up her hand. "About the inheritance, not this so-called murder." And with these words, she was off, clutching her Chanel purse under her arms, looking like a woman with not a single care in the world.

Odelia sighed. If only she could exude so much class!

※

The day of Harriet's photoshoot had finally arrived. The prissy Persian was primped and ready, and not a little excited to give of her best and become the first feline in Hampton Cove to grace the cover of *Cat Life*, only the most popular magazine for cat lovers in the country—perhaps even the world!

The location of the shoot was a studio located on the top floor of Advantage Publishing headquarters, which was a slight disappointment, for Harriet had fully expected the shoot to be an outdoor affair, with some glorious scenery to be displayed behind her. Perhaps the Sahara desert, or the Manhattan skyline.

Instead, they had her in front of a green screen, with the photographer explaining to Odelia and Gran and Scarlett and Marge, who had all decided to be there for this momentous occasion, that they would fill in the background later on. It could be the Eiffel Tower, or the Grand Canyon, or some babbling brook or even an airplane. They hadn't decided yet, which Harriet thought was outrageous.

Then again, the company had just lost its CEO, so perhaps that was the reason they were so ill-prepared.

"I think you look great, sugar pie," said Brutus, who was watching from the sidelines as Harriet got done up to perfection by a professional pet groomer.

"I know I look great," said Harriet as she followed the groomer's progress in the mirror. That spot on her nose was gone, and no other spots had appeared, so it was all good. Except that she felt that her nose didn't look its usual roseate pink but had developed a slight brownish discoloration. Nothing Photoshop wouldn't be able to fix, however—as Brutus kept saying.

"How long is this going to take?" she heard Gran ask. "It's just that we're supposed to be working."

"You're an intern, aren't you?" Harriet snapped. "So that means you're not being paid. Which means you can take as many breaks as you want."

Gran declined to respond, since it would look a little weird in front of the photographer and his team, but she could tell that the old lady couldn't wait to get back to the office, and do whatever it was that she was doing there. Some matchmaking nonsense, if Max was to be believed. Just a lot of silliness, at any rate. What could be more important than this photoshoot? Nothing!

"Just sit back and enjoy," said the groomer as she powdered Harriet's nose. "This is your moment, sweetie. This is the day you're going to be immortalized!"

And so she sat back and tried to relax. This was her moment. Her big moment!

I was watching the scene with a sort of detachment. My mind was whirring with potential suspects and possible scenarios of how Michael Madison could have met such a sticky end. Odelia had told us about her brief interview with Deith Madison, and how she had checked with the woman's boyfriend, who'd confirmed her alibi. So that was one less suspect to consider, which unfortunately didn't make things easier for us.

We'd already come to the conclusion that Tom Mitchell was our guy, considering his habit of chucking people he didn't like out of windows. But a second visit to Melanie Mitchell had only met with the latter's firm reiteration of her earlier statement that Tom had been home that night—all night.

So he couldn't have done it either. Unless Melanie was lying, of course.

"She looks gorgeous, doesn't she?" said Brutus with a sort of whimpering adulation. "These pictures are for the kids."

"What kids?" I asked. "You guys don't have kids."

Brutus winced. "Please keep your voice down!"

"But it's true," I said. "You're neutered and Harriet is spayed."

"We could always adopt," he said.

"But—"

"For God's sakes, Max, don't spoil Harriet's finest hour!"

"Okay, fine," I said. "Forget I said anything."

"I will. Now please be quiet. This is her moment. Her moment to shine."

And shine, she did. The groomer had finished prepping her to within an inch of her life, and she had never looked better—or more unnatural. Her fur had a sort of shine to it, which very likely came from a bottle, and her face was lit up.

"She's glowing, isn't she, Max?" said Dooley. "She's actually glowing."

"Glowing from all the junk they've put on her," I grumbled.

Okay, so I wasn't in a good mood. Can you blame me? My human had asked me to assist her in cracking this case, and so far all I'd done was move around in circles, not getting any closer to the truth. It was frustrating, to say the least.

The photographer had been getting ready, placing several cameras on a table. I wondered why he needed so many of them. A cover picture is just that: one picture. But as I was about to find out, before he selected the perfect picture, he was going to take dozens and dozens of them. Hundreds, perhaps. And Harriet was sitting through them with perfect —and uncustomary—patience.

During a break in the proceedings, which was necessary to touch up Harriet's makeup, the photog sauntered over in our direction. "I heard you guys are looking into what happened to Mike?" he said, addressing Odelia.

"Yeah, we're trying to find out how he died," Odelia confirmed.

"Good luck with that," said the photographer, who was a thirty-something male with a ponytail, a long black beard, and plenty of tattoos on his arms and neck. "From what I heard there were no witnesses, so who knows what happened."

"Did you know Mike Madison?" asked Odelia, who never missed an opportunity to talk to a potential witness.

"Sure. Mike was always interested in every part of the business. He was in here all the time, sitting in on creative meetings, and even accompanying us on shoots. The guy was a micromanager." He eyed Odelia curiously. "So is it true he was murdered? Only I heard he killed himself, but now rumor has it he was killed."

"At this stage we are treating his death as suspicious," Odelia confirmed.

"Christ," said the guy, sliding a hand along his beard. "This isn't going to do the stock a lot of good. Which isn't going to do any of us any good either."

"You have stock options?"

"Sure. We all have stock options. Only they're probably going to be worthless now, aren't they? Unless you got the kind of options that speculate on the stock dropping, of course. But who would bet on the stock dropping? Not me!"

"How is she doing?" asked Gran, referring to Harriet.

"She's a born model," said the photographer. "A delight to work with. Some photographers hate working with pets. They're hard to handle. Won't sit still, keep shifting position, walk off stage—whatever. But Harriet here is a real pro. Gets the right shot every time. Almost as if she can understand what I say!"

"She probably does," said Gran with a wink.

"Yeah, right." The guy had to laugh at this, even though Gran wasn't kidding.

Harriet was ready for her second round, and the photographer conferred with his art director for a moment, before launching into another series of pictures.

I have to say that the photographer's words touched a chord. It had set the machinery in my noggin shifting into gear, and before long I was lost in thought.

Could it be?

Mh…

CHAPTER 34

The scene at the Mitchells was a happy one. Tom was there, of course, and his little brother Harry and cousin Danny, and his mother Melanie. But more importantly, the scene was set for Natalie Ferrara to arrive in their midst, having agreed to pay a visit to Tom's home, and meet his mother for the first time.

Ever since Tom's initiative in casting Natalie's brother from her home, the two young people had lived through a whirlwind romance that had quickly brought them closer together. Natalie's brother was gone, and had stayed gone, and Natalie's gratefulness was thus that the couple had gone on several dates.

And now the time had come for Natalie to meet Tom's dearest mom.

Everything was in position for the auspicious meeting, with Melanie having put on her best dress for the occasion, and Harry and Danny having pitched in to clean up their home as best they could. Harry had handled the vacuum cleaner, and Danny the duster, and together they'd turned the house into a picture of domestic cleanliness.

Meanwhile, Melanie had been busy in the kitchen, preparing a delicious meal. Spring potatoes were on the menu, and veal and peas, with homemade cheesecake for dessert. She just hoped Tom's new girlfriend would like it. He was nervous enough himself, and not in the mood for a lot of questions, even though she had been peppering him with them, and so had Harry and Danny.

Finally the doorbell chimed and Melanie wiped her hands on her apron, then took it off and draped it over a kitchen chair. "She's here!" she announced as she hurried into the living room. She glanced round, and saw that the place looked better than it had looked in years, with Harry and Danny standing at attention.

Tom had already gone into the hallway to open the door to his great love. But when he returned, it wasn't Natalie Ferrara accompanying him but that reporter woman, Odelia Kingsley, and a big, burly male who looked like a cop. Behind them, two cats trailed. The fat orange one the reporter had brought along last time, and a fluffy gray one.

The big guy flashed a badge. "Detective Chase Kingsley," he said. "Hampton Cove PD."

She blinked. "What's going on?" she demanded. "Where is Natalie?" And then it hit her, and she clutched both hands to her face. "Oh, dear God, no. Not again! Did something happen to Natalie? Did she have an accident? Tell me it isn't true!"

"Natalie is fine," the Kingsley woman assured her. "We're not here about her."

"So what are you here for?" asked Melanie, confused. "I don't understand."

"I think you better take a seat, Mrs. Mitchell," said Mrs. Kingsley. "In fact why don't we all take a seat?"

Melanie plunked herself down on the couch, staring at the twosome. "What is this?" she asked. "What happened?"

"I'm afraid we're both here in an official capacity, Mrs. Mitchell," said the cop. "Odelia here is a police consultant, and I'm the detective in charge of the investigation into the murder of Michael Madison."

"Again with this murder business? What's that got to do with us?" She glanced to her eldest, but Tom seemed as stunned by this development as she was.

"Because at this stage of the proceedings," said the detective, "I think we have a fairly accurate idea of what happened that night."

"You see," the Kingsley woman said, "all this time we were looking at people who held a grudge against Michael, but instead we should have been looking for the people who had something to gain from his death. So you might say we were looking in the wrong direction, which is exactly what the murderer wanted."

"There were plenty of people who held a grudge against Madison," Detective Kingsley continued. "But not that many who had anything to gain. In fact the only person who benefited from Michael Madison's death was an investor."

"An investor?" asked Melanie. "I don't understand."

"It took us a while to see the full picture ourselves," said Mrs. Kingsley. "You see, every employee of the Advantage Publishing Company is given stock options when they sign their contract. It's up to them if they choose to take advantage of those options, but most do. Of course you want the stock of the company to go up, in which case your options will increase in value. Not down, reducing the value."

"Okay," said Melanie, wondering what they were talking about.

"But there is a different kind of option," said the detective. "It's called a put option, and it speculates that the stock of a company will go down. In other words decrease in value. The more the stock drops, the bigger the gain. And since options work on the principle of leverage, the value increase of the put option is many times greater than the value decrease of the stock."

"Typically when the CEO of a company dies, or as in this case seemingly commits suicide, it will send the stock plummeting," Mrs. Kingsley continued the complicated tale. "And in the case of Advantage, that's exactly what happened. The day after Madison's apparent suicide, Advantage stock dropped twenty percent. Which isn't so strange, since investors don't like uncertainty. At the same time, though, the investor with the put options made a quite spectacular return."

"Uh-huh," said Melanie. It all sounded like Chinese to her. She turned to Harry. "Do you understand anything the detective just said, Harry?" She explained, "Harry is the brainy one. Always hacking things. Isn't that right, Harry?"

"How many times do we have to tell you, Mom," said Tom. "Harry isn't a hacker. He's an investor. He buys and sells stock on his… computer." Suddenly Tom's eyes widened, even as Harry's eyes dipped to the carpet, and a blush suffused his face.

A pregnant pause fell, and all eyes turned to Harry.

"Harry?" said Melanie, as something tightened in her throat. "What is this?"

"Nothing, Mom," Harry muttered, but she could see her youngest was lying.

"Harry! What did you do?!" she demanded.

But Harry only seemed to shrink more into himself.

"I'm afraid your son Harry has been speculating on a decrease of Advantage Publishing stock," said Detective Kingsley. "The day before Michael Madison died, he invested all his previous winnings into put options, effectively betting that Advantage stock would drop. The day after Michael died, he executed those options, netting himself an impressive gain of one hundred thousand dollars."

Melanie's jaw dropped. "One hundred thousand!"

"The only reason he could have known that Michael would die, is if he had a hand in his death himself."

"But he never left the house," Melanie said. "None of my boys did." She realized as she said it, how unconvincing her words sounded, even to her own ears.

"Are you sure about that, Melanie?" asked Odelia Kingsley gently.

Melanie swallowed, then said hesitantly, "Yes?"

"Let me tell you what we think happened," said the detective. "When his cousin told him about this whole business with the stock options, Harry smelled an opportunity to make some good money. So he and Danny devised a plan. A couple of days before the murder, Danny, who knows the building inside and out, managed to get a hold of Madison's badge, and handed it to Harry, who was waiting in the parking lot. Harry cloned the badge on his computer, and Danny quickly returned the original badge before Madison found out it was missing.

"So the night of the murder, Danny snuck into the building using the cloned badge, which is why security thought the only person in the building was Madison. Danny snuck up to Madison's office, knowing all about the man's habit of working late into the night. He entered the office when Madison's back was turned, overpowered him and shoved him out of the window. He then used the same badge to exit the building and check the man's vital signs to make sure he was dead. Then he went home to give his cousin the good news."

Danny's eyes had gone wide. "But how do you know all this?!" he cried, getting up. But he sank down on the couch again, realizing he'd just given himself away.

"You idiot!" Harry yelled. "You stupid, stupid idiot!"

"Harry?" said Melanie, a tremor in her voice. "Tell me this isn't true."

Harry shrugged. "You're always complaining about money, Mom. How you can't pay for this or that or whatever. So I just figured we could use the money to pay off the mortgage. Own the house free and clear, never having to worry again."

"But Harry—killing a man? How could you?"

"He was a corporate rat, Mom. The same kind of corporate rat who are always threatening to kick us out of our house. So instead of them screwing us over, I decided to screw him over for a change. And it worked. It actually worked."

"Oh, Harry," she said, crumpling like a used tissue.

Tom had to support her, or she would have fallen to the floor.

The doorbell rang a second time, and Mrs. Kingsley went to open it. Natalie Ferrara walked in, but if she had expected to find a happy scene, she was sorely disappointed. Instead, she walked in on an arrest in progress, with both Harry and Danny Mitchell being apprehended for the murder of Michael Madison.

And so what was supposed to be the happiest day in Melanie Mitchell's life, turned out to be one of the darkest ones instead.

CHAPTER 35

"The thing I should have asked myself," I explained, "was the basic question any detective should always ask themselves: who stood to gain from Michael Madison's death. But instead we all focused on who simply wanted him dead."

"I think you did great, Max," said Brutus. "You got there in the end, and that's all that matters."

We were seated on the porch swing in Marge and Tex's backyard, the four of us lined up in a row. We'd eaten a nice meal, consisting of not-so-vegetarian pieces of chicken filet, and now we were relaxing and doing some people watching.

"I could have gotten there sooner," I said. "But who would have thought a fifteen-year-old and his cousin would be behind this whole sordid business?"

"And Danny seemed like such a nice kid," said Dooley. "I really liked him."

"I think we all liked him. He was very helpful and kind. But he was also a killer, and one thing doesn't seem to exclude the other."

"Poor Tom," said Dooley. "Now that he finally got the girl, he's lost his brother and his cousin."

"Yeah, tough," I agreed. Though Natalie would be a great support for Melanie, who had taken the arrest of her son and nephew hard, as was to be expected.

"Harry did it to help his mom," said Harriet. "And besides, he's a minor, so the judge will probably go easy on him."

"Even if he did it to help his mom," I said, "murder is still murder, Harriet."

"I know, I know." All this talk about murder had distracted attention from her photoshoot, and she didn't like it. She glanced over to the humans, and when she saw they were also discussing the murder, she slumped. "This was supposed to be the best moment of my life—and you ruined it, Max! You and your murder!"

"It wasn't my murder, Harriet," I pointed out.

"Yeah, I know," she said moodily. "But nobody is going to care about my cover now. It's all going to be about Madison and the terrible things that happened."

"I'm sure by the time the copy of *Cat Life* with your cover comes out," I said, "people will have forgotten all about this murder business."

She perked up at this. "You think?"

"Of course. And I'm sure Marge and Odelia will buy up several copies, and frame your cover and give it pride of place in their homes."

"Oh, I would like that so much," she said, clasping her paws together. "They could hang one in the living room, and one in the bedroom, and one in the bathroom. And the toilet, of course. Very important. So they can study my portrait when they're doing their business."

Somehow the notion of having to look at Harriet when I'm doing my business didn't appeal to me all that much. Then again, humans are different. They probably love looking at the portrait of a pretty Persian when they go to the smallest room in the house.

"So how long are you going to keep working for Advantage?" asked Charlene as she leafed through a copy of *Glimmer*, which seemed to have become her favorite magazine.

"We stopped working last week," said Gran. "Tex needs me," she explained. "And besides, our work was done."

Tex didn't look like he particularly needed Gran, but since he was busy working the grill, he wasn't in a position to protest.

"We got Tom and Natalie together," said Scarlett, "and so Gabi's job is finished."

"Are you going to go undercover in every situation where people need Gabi's assistance?" asked Uncle Alec.

"Who knows?" said Gran, darting a glance at her friend. "We haven't discussed it yet, but it was definitely an interesting experience."

"Yeah, I feel invigorated," Scarlett agreed.

"It's nice to be needed, especially at our age," said Gran.

"Oh, if you're looking for a job, you can always work for me," said Charlene. "My secretary is always complaining I give her too much to do. So you could give her a hand."

"Or you could work for me," said Marge. "There's always work at the library."

"No, thanks," said Gran. "Like I said, Tex needs me. And I'm sure pretty soon another interesting letter will come in for Gabi, and then Scarlett and I can work our magic once more. We're getting pretty good at this stuff, aren't we, honey?"

"Absolutely," said Scarlett. "And I like this a lot better than the neighborhood watch business." She touched her face. "A girl needs her beauty sleep, and the watch was cutting into my sleep."

"Same here," said Gran, as she yawned and stretched.

"Well, I'm glad to hear it," said Uncle Alec, who had never been a big fan of the neighborhood watch. "Police business should be handled by trained professionals only, not by amateurs like you," he admonished his mother and her friend.

"Yeah, yeah, yeah," said Gran. She darted a glance at her son-in-law and lowered her voice. "So is everything all right with you guys?"

Marge nodded. "Absolutely," she said. "In fact things have never been better."

"Good to know," said Gran, settling back. "Looks like all's well that ends well."

And as we watched from our perch on the porch, we saw how Charlene held up her copy of *Glimmer*, then handed it to Uncle Alec. A silent communication passed between the couple, and moments later Charlene excused herself and removed herself from the select company, soon followed by Uncle Alec.

Marge picked up the magazine and checked the article Charlene had been reading. "15 More Ways to Spice Up Your Love Life," she read, then darted a keen look in her husband's direction.

I closed my eyes for just a few moments, but when I opened them again, Marge and Tex were gone, and Odelia was reading that same article. She handed it to Chase, who grinned and whispered, "Are you thinking what I'm thinking?" And before I knew it, they were heading through the opening in the hedge, hand in hand like a couple of lovebirds, and skedaddled!

"Where did all the humans go?" asked Harriet, who had noticed the same phenomenon.

"Uncle Alec and Charlene are in those bushes over there," said Dooley, who had kept his eyes peeled. "Marge and Tex went into the house. And Odelia and Chase went home."

The only ones left were Gran and Scarlett. And Grace, of course, who was studying a flower, and ripping off its petals, possibly playing a game of 'He loves me, he loves me not.'

Gran and Scarlett shared a look of satisfaction. "That article you wrote is a big hit," Gran said, picking up the magazine.

"Of course it is," said Scarlett. "I could write a dozen articles like that."

"You know? I think I could get used to this."

"What?"

"Well, spreading sweetness and light, you know."

"Me too. I like making people happy. It makes me feel good inside."

"It does, doesn't it? Makes you feel all warm and fuzzy. I say from now on we focus on the business of spreading joy and happiness in the world."

"Hear, hear."

"Who else can we make happy?"

They both thought for a moment.

"Marcie and Ted from next door?" Scarlett suggested.

"They seem happy enough," said Gran sadly.

"Kurt Mayfield?" Scarlett said, referring to Odelia and Chase's neighbor.

"Nobody likes a lost cause," Gran grumbled.

Then I happened to catch Gran's eye, and I could see her eyes widen as an idea struck that buzzing brain of hers.

"No," I said immediately. "No way."

"Shanille is single," said Gran, perking up.

"Please leave me alone," I said.

"And so are dozens of other nice girls."

"Absolutely not!" I cried, hopping down from the porch.

"Maybe Max is gay," Scarlett said. "Or maybe he likes dogs."

"I'm not gay, and I don't like dogs!" I yelled, starting to panic.

"Why don't you let us set you up on a nice date, mh?" said Gran.

"I don't want a date!" I cried, looking for a way out of this nightmare.

"I like dates, Max," said Dooley. "They're sweet and contain lots of fiber."

"Come with me, Dooley," I said urgently, as I started removing myself from the scene. "If you know what's good for you, you will come with me right now! And whatever you do, don't look into their eyes!"

"Max! Dooley!" Gran yelled. "Come back here! Let us spice up your life! It's what we do!"

THE END

Thanks for reading! If you want to know when a new Nic Saint book comes out, sign up for Nic's mailing list: nicsaint.com/news

ABOUT NIC

Nic has a background in political science and before being struck by the writing bug worked odd jobs around the world (including but not limited to massage therapist in Mexico, gardener in Italy, restaurant manager in India, and Berlitz teacher in Belgium).

When he's not writing he enjoys curling up with a good (comic) book, watching British crime dramas, French comedies or Nancy Meyers movies, sampling pastry (apple cake!), pasta and chocolate (preferably the dark variety), twisting himself into a pretzel doing morning yoga, going for a run, and spoiling his big red tomcat Tommy.

He lives with his wife (and aforementioned cat) in a small village smack dab in the middle of absolutely nowhere and is probably writing his next 'Mysteries of Max' book right now.

www.nicsaint.com

ALSO BY NIC SAINT

The Mysteries of Max

Purrfect Murder

Purrfectly Deadly

Purrfect Revenge

Purrfect Heat

Purrfect Crime

Purrfect Rivalry

Purrfect Peril

Purrfect Secret

Purrfect Alibi

Purrfect Obsession

Purrfect Betrayal

Purrfectly Clueless

Purrfectly Royal

Purrfect Cut

Purrfect Trap

Purrfectly Hidden

Purrfect Kill

Purrfect Boy Toy

Purrfectly Dogged

Purrfectly Dead

Purrfect Saint

Purrfect Advice

Purrfect Passion

A Purrfect Gnomeful

Purrfect Cover

Purrfect Patsy

Purrfect Son

Purrfect Fool

Purrfect Fitness

Purrfect Setup

Purrfect Sidekick

Purrfect Deceit

Purrfect Ruse

Purrfect Swing

Purrfect Cruise

Purrfect Harmony

Purrfect Sparkle

Purrfect Cure

Purrfect Cheat

Purrfect Catch

Purrfect Design

Purrfect Life

Purrfect Thief

Purrfect Crust

Purrfect Bachelor

Purrfect Double

Purrfect Date

Purrfect Hit

Purrfect Baby

Purrfect Mess

Purrfect Paris

Purrfect Model
Purrfect Slug
Purrfect Match

The Mysteries of Max Box Sets

Box Set 1 (Books 1-3)
Box Set 2 (Books 4-6)
Box Set 3 (Books 7-9)
Box Set 4 (Books 10-12)
Box Set 5 (Books 13-15)
Box Set 6 (Books 16-18)
Box Set 7 (Books 19-21)
Box Set 8 (Books 22-24)
Box Set 9 (Books 25-27)
Box Set 10 (Books 28-30)
Box Set 11 (Books 31-33)
Box Set 12 (Books 34-36)
Box Set 13 (Books 37-39)
Box Set 14 (Books 40-42)
Box Set 15 (Books 43-45)
Box Set 16 (Books 46-48)
Box Set 17 (Books 49-51)

The Mysteries of Max Big Box Sets

Big Box Set 1 (Books 1-10)
Big Box Set 2 (Books 11-20)

The Mysteries of Max Shorts

Purrfect Santa (3 shorts in one)
Purrfectly Flealess

Purrfect Wedding
Purrfect Fuzz
Purrfect Love

Nora Steel

Murder Retreat

The Kellys

Murder Motel
Death in Suburbia

Emily Stone

Murder at the Art Class

Washington & Jefferson

First Shot

Alice Whitehouse

Spooky Times
Spooky Trills
Spooky End
Spooky Spells

Ghosts of London

Between a Ghost and a Spooky Place
Public Ghost Number One
Ghost Save the Queen
Box Set 1 (Books 1-3)
A Tale of Two Harrys
Ghost of Girlband Past
Ghostlier Things

Charleneland

Deadly Ride

Final Ride

Neighborhood Witch Committee

Witchy Start

Witchy Worries

Witchy Wishes

Saffron Diffley

Crime and Retribution

Vice and Verdict

Felonies and Penalties (Saffron Diffley Short 1)

The B-Team

Once Upon a Spy

Tate-à-Tate

Enemy of the Tates

Ghosts vs. Spies

The Ghost Who Came in from the Cold

Witchy Fingers

Witchy Trouble

Witchy Hexations

Witchy Possessions

Witchy Riches

Box Set 1 (Books 1-4)

The Mysteries of Bell & Whitehouse

One Spoonful of Trouble

Two Scoops of Murder

Three Shots of Disaster

Box Set 1 (Books 1-3)

A Twist of Wraith

A Touch of Ghost

A Clash of Spooks

Box Set 2 (Books 4-6)

The Stuffing of Nightmares

A Breath of Dead Air

An Act of Hodd

Box Set 3 (Books 7-9)

A Game of Dons

Standalone Novels

When in Bruges

The Whiskered Spy

ThrillFix

Homejacking

The Eighth Billionaire

The Wrong Woman

Made in United States
Troutdale, OR
09/28/2023

13240450R00137